Totally Bound Publis}

Sin

Sun, Sta

CW00742098

SUN, STARS & LIMONCELLO

STEFANIA HARTLEY

Sun, Stars & Limoncello
ISBN # 978-1-83943-901-8
©Copyright Stefania Hartley 2020
Cover Art by Louisa Maggio ©Copyright July 2020
Interior text design by Claire Siemaszkiewicz
Totally Bound Publishing

SUN, STARS & LIMONCELLO

Dedication

To all the people who believe that they don't
deserve love anymore.

Chapter One

Sonia felt like she'd sped straight into a wall, even though the broken leg wasn't hers. Kate would not be coming on the trip. The staffroom was plunged into silence as the other teachers pondered the impact that their colleague's sick leave would have on them.

"Then there's the Sicily school trip to cover," Mrs. Ashcroft continued, "because even though we all know that Sonia would happily take twenty-eight Year Sevens to Sicily all by herself…"

Yes, she wouldn't think twice about taking the kids on the trip on her own. She'd do anything for them. She curled her fingers tighter around her mug.

"It wouldn't be legal. Our school cook and his wife are going with her, but we need another teacher. Unless, Sonia, you wish to cancel the trip?" Mrs. Ashcroft turned to her and all her colleagues' eyes swiveled in her direction.

Cancel the trip? After her students had worked incredibly hard on their Italian, baked and sold cakes and washed cars to raise money? She had fought tooth and nail for the grants that would allow even the less-well-off to come. Then there was Charlotte Rogers, who had fixed her with her big, sad eyes and thanked her for this trip, because it would give her respite from her warring parents. *No, I can't cancel it!* She wouldn't, even if she had to pay someone to go with her. "Absolutely not," she answered resolutely.

"Then we need a volunteer to go with Sonia," Mrs. Ashcroft confirmed, scanning the staffroom. Bums shifted on chairs, hands crept to watches and the wind whistled outside the windows. All eyes were pinned to the floor except one green pair. Even though she didn't dare look in that direction, Sonia felt them on her.

No, not him. Please, not him.

"The kids going are a lovely bunch of Year Sevens," Sonia said, trying in vain to make eye contact with her other colleagues, "and Sicily is very beautiful in April — not too cold, not too hot."

Eventually, Rachel looked up. "I'm sorry, Sonia. I'd love to come, but I haven't got anyone to look after my kids."

Mildred explained that her knees were giving her trouble and she couldn't walk far. Alistair had just had his first baby. Grumpy old John muttered some excuse. Anyway, Sonia knew that he wouldn't give the school a minute more than his contracted time. Chantelle had already booked her Eurostar ticket home, and Sonia delicately avoided sending a glance in Bernie's direction. During the holidays, she'd be going for another IVF attempt. One after the other, all the remaining teachers declined the invitation. When even the head felt the need to excuse herself — a crucial meeting with the school governors — Sonia felt her last drop of hope drip away.

The only member of staff left was the owner of the jade eyes that had followed her from the beginning of the staff briefing, but Sonia avoided looking anywhere near that direction. She had absolutely no wish to travel with him, and she was utterly confident that her feelings were fully reciprocated. Brad Wilson had gotten under her skin like a freezing cold shower from the day he had started at the school. He seemed to have no normal, friendly way to look at her. He either averted his gaze or pinned her with one of his icy stares — unsmiling, as if he were about to dish her a detention. The first few times, she had checked her reflection in a window. Was her décolleté too low? Her skirt too short? Eventually, she had concluded that he was just a miserable wet blanket.

She could put up with Brad Wilson in other circumstances but not on this trip. She had cajoled the newlywed cook, Jake, to come along with his wife, only under the promise that it would be as close to the honeymoon they hadn't been able to afford as she could make it. When Kate had been going with her, Sonia hadn't minded the idea of giving the couple space, provided they were available in the event of an emergency. But if Brad took Kate's place, the setup would be much too much like a double date. The idea was totally cringeworthy, especially as there wasn't a single female member of staff who wouldn't swoon over Brad Wilson.

Not that she was in any way attracted to him. *No way*. She was done with men. *Made the mistake, got the T-shirt, learned the lesson*. But being pushed together with the staff's heartthrob would be uncomfortable, if not utterly unpleasant.

Sonia felt his brooding presence and, out of the corners of her eyes, she could make out his tall figure leaned against the door jamb, detached from the rest of the staff, his mug in one hand, laptop carelessly held under his other arm. She kept her gaze trained on the ground, but she could feel his gaze needling her. *Do not make eye contact. Do not look at him or at anything near him.* If she could have made a sign flash on her forehead with the words *Brad Wilson need not apply*, she would have.

"How about you, Brad? Could *you* go with Sonia?"

Mrs. Ashcroft's words made time slow down and blur like a bullet in the movies, only there was no way Sonia could dodge this bullet if he said yes.

Please, say no. You must have a holiday booked, a girlfriend waiting or a wife and children at home. Please, be busy.

He clutched the mug to his chest like it was a miniature shield and contorted his face into a pained frown.

Please, say no. Make up an excuse.

"I suppose I should." He sighed.

A flood of angry adrenaline restarted Sonia's internal time at a galloping trot. That was the unkindest acceptance he could have ever conjured up. '*I suppose I should.*' Was there a more convincing way to make it clear beyond a doubt that they were twisting his oh-so-handsome-and-muscly arm? He was going to oblige, but only out of duty, and he would do it with as little grace as possible — and even less enthusiasm.

Before Sonia had a chance to refuse his 'offer', Mrs. Ashcroft replied hastily, "Thank you, Brad. That's very kind of you."

'*Kind*' was the last word Sonia would have used to describe Brad Wilson.

Brad immediately regretted agreeing to go on the trip. He could have given plenty of reasons to excuse himself—the GCSE revision sessions, the A-level experiments that needed daily monitoring, the trainee teachers' appraisals and lots of other stuff.

And he hated school trips. Being surrounded by people around-the-clock was his idea of torture. He needed his regular fixes of solitude and silence, which he was unlikely to get on a school trip, where keeping the kids in their rooms—let alone in their beds—would be a game of Whack-a-Mole. But the main—and crucial—reason why he should have refused to accompany that trip was *her*.

There was something about the olive-skinned modern languages teacher that unsettled him. And unsettling was the last thing he needed. He needed peace. He didn't need women, emotions and heartache. He had sworn to himself that he would never let his heart be shredded by grief again. A self-contained, self-sufficient life, without joys or sorrows, was the way forward for him. It was all he could cope with.

He knew well that you couldn't cut scar tissue over and over again and expect it to heal. His heart had already been ripped to smithereens. All he could do to protect it was not get attached to another person ever again. If he did just that, the worst tragedy that could ever happen to him would be his own death—and that was something he often yearned for.

But Sonia was the opposite of death. As well as her own, she seemed to have been granted his share of *joie de vivre* too. She was a heart pulsating with life, worn on the sleeve of her flowery dresses. Everyone loved her and she had forged great relationships with everyone on the staff—except him. He had kept her at a distance because, to him, she was pure, distilled danger.

He had prayed that one of their colleagues would volunteer to go on the trip, both for her sake and for the children's. Most of the students were in his science class, and they hadn't been able to talk about anything but Miss Alletti's Sicily trip for weeks. They'd be crushed if it was canceled. As, one by one, their colleagues had made their excuses, he'd had the urge to step forward, but had stopped himself. How could he keep his distance from Sonia if they were pushed together for an entire week? But when Mrs. Ashcroft had asked him, he hadn't felt that he could refuse, even if that meant traveling with a woman who made his breath stop in his chest each time they crossed paths in the corridor.

* * * *

As soon as Mrs. Ashcroft had moved on to the next agenda item, Sonia snuck out of the staffroom through the fire exit and huddled under the corrugated iron roof of the bicycle shed — where truants and smokers went. There, she secretly rang the two teachers who hadn't been at the briefing because they worked part-time. They were her last hope for a replacement, which faded as quickly as a puff of smoke, as neither was available on such short notice. Her choices were a trip with Brad or no trip at all, which wasn't an option. For the love of her children, she would have to put up with him. She straightened her back, clutched her laptop to her chest and set off down the corridor to her first lesson.

"*Buon giorno*, Miss Alletti. How are you?" Ryan welcomed her at the door.

"Uhm… *Buona domanda*, good question."

"*Buon giorno*, Miss Alletti," all the other Year Sevens chorused, scuttling to their seats as soon as she crossed the classroom's threshold.

Their lovely smiles reminded Sonia of why she loved her job. "*Buon giorno*, Year Sevens."

There was a moment of expectant silence, then Charlotte Rogers said, "You've forgotten the bit that goes, 'and what a good day it will be'."

Yes, she always said that. She just hadn't realized that they remembered it. "That's right. And a good day today it will be too, even if it didn't start very well."

"What happened, Miss?" Ryan asked.

Sonia plugged her laptop into the docking station and leaned against her desk. "The trip was almost canceled."

Horrified gasps rippled through the classroom.

"But it wasn't," she hastily added. "Mrs. Johnstone has broken her leg and can't come anymore but"—she hesitated—"Mr. Wilson has agreed to come in her place."

"Yay!"

"Yes, yes, yes!"

"He's our science teacher, Miss!" the class cheered.

This was not the reaction Sonia had expected. She had imagined groans and protestations, like when the nurse came to give them their yearly jabs. Instead, it was more like the reaction to snow days. Did they *like* Mr. Wilson?

Just then, there was a rap on the door. Before she had time to answer, a figure appeared on the threshold. *Speak of the devil*. The class roared and he looked a little startled, which was a change from his default frown.

"We were just talking about you," Sonia explained.

"You're coming on the trip with us, Mr. Wilson?" Aidan shouted.

"It seems so," he said, the hint of a smile curling his lips.

Where had his hauteur and coldness gone?

"Can you speak Italian, Mr. Wilson?" Charlotte asked.

"Apart from *ciao*, *pizza* and *pasta*, no." His face broke into an actual smile, something Sonia had never seen on him before. It was a really nice smile, with dimples and cute little folds of skin under the eyes.

"Don't worry, Mr. Wilson. We'll translate for you."

"Better still if you teach me." There was a hint of sweetness in his voice that gave Sonia goosebumps. Was this the same snobbish head of biology who shot steely glances at her and never deigned to indulge her with a word? He must be one of those teachers who were lovely with children but cold with other adults — or maybe he was only cold to her.

"I will! I will!" various children cried out.

Sonia felt a prick of jealousy at her class's display of affection. "What can we do for you, Mr. Wilson?" she interrupted briskly.

"I've come to ask whether you need me to fill in any paperwork for the trip," he said, catapulting himself back to his usual formality and distance.

"I need a copy of your passport for the travel agent," she replied, just as formally.

"Will do." If he had shouted *yessir* and clacked his heels together, it wouldn't have looked out of place. He then nodded a goodbye to the class and turned to go.

"See you on Saturday, Mr. Wilson!" Aidan shouted.

"See you, Mr. Wilson!" the others echoed.

Sonia immediately recalled the class's attention. "Today we'll learn to talk about our hobbies," she said in a voice brittle with annoyance.

"What's your favorite hobby, Miss?" Laura Hardman asked.

"I love swimming," she replied.

"Mr. Wilson's hobby is sailing," Aidan volunteered.

"He's not just hot, then," Charlotte said, putting her mascara back in her pencil case.

"No. He's a sailing instructor too," Aidan pressed on. "Can you sail, Miss Alletti?"

"Alas, no." She hoped that her sarcasm wasn't obvious to anyone but her.

"And Mr. Wilson can play football too," Aidan continued.

"He's Mr.-Wonderful-Wilson," some of the girls said, doe-eyed.

Sonia couldn't roll her eyes in front of her students, but a secret groan rose up in her chest.

* * * *

"If Kate isn't coming, are you canceling the trip?" Her mum's face was a dark shadow on the phone's screen and Sonia made a mental note to tell her that she should avoid being backlit in a videocall.

"No. I've got someone to replace her." Sonia squatted to pull the small pot out of the kitchen cupboard. She could have just stretched her arm, but she suddenly felt the need to hide from her mother's gaze.

"Who's that?"

"Another colleague." Sonia emerged with the pot but switched to English to avoid the masculine and feminine nouns in Italian.

"*Una collega o un collega*?" her mum carried on in Italian.

Sonia dunked the pot in the sink and turned on the tap until the water roared. "*Un collega.*"

"What did you say?" her mom asked.

She turned off the tap. "*Un collega,*" she mumbled.

"Ah."

There was a meaningful pause, which Sonia purposefully ignored.

"Is he single?" Her mum's voice was now intense and focused, in full-on matchmaking mode, she knew.

"I don't know."

"Why? You've been at that school since September and still don't know?" She tutted. "How old is he?"

"Does the order of the questions mean that age is less of an issue than marital status?"

"I don't understand you."

"I'm asking if you'd rather an elderly bachelor accompanied me on the trip rather than a married young man."

"Of course! Never mess around with married men. You know what happened to Mariolina—"

"I know what happened to Mariolina, but things have changed, Mamma. Being a married man's lover doesn't make you an outcast from society anymore."

"Heaven forbid, Sonia! Please tell me that you keep clear of married men."

"Of course, I do—"

"*Brava.*"

"Because I keep clear of all men."

Her mum's disapproving silence and cocked eyebrow lasted so long that Sonia had time to put the pot on the hob, find the matching lid and turn on the fire.

"Maybe your father and I were a little too strict about boyfriends when you were younger, but now you're old enough to look for a man, my darling. You have all our blessings."

Sonia whipped around to the fridge, turning her back on her mum. She didn't want to talk about the things that had happened when she'd been younger. But she didn't need anything from the fridge, so she closed it again. Being British as well as Sicilian, she changed the topic to the weather. "It should be nice in Palermo this time of year."

"But it'll be colder in the mountains. And don't forget mosquito repellent."

"Good idea—"

"Have you got your toothbrush?" her mom asked.

"Yes—"

"One pair of underpants for each day?"

"You're talking to me as if I were a child." Her mum just didn't seem to understand that there could be a whole life between being a child and becoming a bride. But then, how could she? She had been handed over from her father to her husband all those years ago. "Enough about me. How are you?"

"Like any old person."

"You're barely fifty."

"I feel old."

"You'd feel better if you did some exercise."

"I know. I know. I need to lose weight. But, no matter how fat and ugly I am, your father will never cheat on me. He still loves me."

"You're not doing it for him, Mum. Women don't do stuff only to please men." The pasta water was boiling. Sonia flung the pasta into the pot and dropped too much salt in.

"For their children too, of course."

"Not only—"

"Then, who for?"

She just doesn't get it.

"Themselves."

"Ah, no. That would be selfish."

The salt made the boiling water foam over the rim and pour all down the sides of the pot. Sonia sighed. "Got to go, Mamma."

"You put too much salt in the water. *Ciao.*"

Sonia closed the call then finished and drained the pasta, wiped up the mess and sat at the breakfast table to eat her dinner. Her mum's ideas wouldn't have been out of place in a Victorian convent school. Her entire life had revolved around the whims of her husband, and she had kept nothing for herself, not even her own body. But—Sonia reflected as she chewed a mouthful of salty spaghetti—her mum never ate alone.

* * * *

The following day Sonia had to endure again her Year Sevens waxing lyrical about Mr.-Wonderful-Wilson. Someone even went as far as swearing that they'd seen his photo in the Africa section of *The Economist* magazine, at which Charlotte shouted, "I knew he must be a model!"

So, instead of taking her break in the staffroom, as she usually did when she wasn't on playground duty, Sonia holed up in the broom-cupboard-sized languages office. At least there was no chance that Mr.-Marvelous-Wilson would rear his ugly head in that windowless place.

To be fair, there was not a trace of ugliness about his head—or any other part of his body. It was actually a rather fine head, especially when he smiled and it was firmly screwed on an equally fine body, both of which would have made Michelangelo proud. But that certainly wasn't a point in Mr.-Marvelous-Wilson's favor. Sonia was done with men — and handsome ones above all. She didn't want anything to do with those. The last time she had fallen for one, her world had come tumbling down. Twelve years later, she still had nightmares and a hollow feeling in the pit of her stomach each time she thought about… *Oh, God, I was only sixteen!*

The French teacher, Chantelle, burst into the room. "Ah, Sonia, here you are. Brad left this for you." She handed her a passport. "He said that you can leave it in his pigeonhole in the staffroom when you've finished with it. You lucky thing, going on the trip with him." Chantelle winked mischievously.

Sonia rolled her eyes. "Believe you me, I would much rather go with Kate." She slapped the passport on the desk and plonked herself on the chair.

"Whatever you think of him, it's good to have a male teacher with you when you're taking boys on a trip. And he's medically trained too, from the rumors I've heard. *Merde*, I'm late for playground duty. Got to go… Bye."

'Medically trained' sounded useful. *What kind of medical training?* Before Sonia could ask, Chantelle was gone. *Bah!* She probably meant that he was a qualified first-aider.

Sonia sank lower in her chair and took a luxuriously long sip from her mug. *Ah, peace at last.* The next person who disturbed her and mentioned the wonders of Mr.-Wonderful-Wilson would get more than an eye-roll from her.

She picked up the passport. It was well-worn and thick with visa stickers. Mr.-Wonderful-Wilson must have been affected by '*wander*lust'. She leafed through the pages. Sierra Leone… Tajikistan… Haiti…

Uganda... Mozambique... Ah, that must be why he wasn't keen on her trip. Sicily wasn't exotic enough for Mr.-Wealthy-Wilson! She imagined him on an exclusive safari, with his tanned muscly legs in khaki shorts. She shook the thought out of her head and studied the date stamps instead.

Kenya—entry April 14, 2018, exit April 28, 2018. *So, clearly a safari.*

Haiti—entry January 23, 2010, exit February 27, 2010. *Winter sunshine, no doubt.*

Sierra Leone—entry December 14, 2014, exit March 20, 2015. *Whoa, what a luxuriously long Christmas break.*

He couldn't possibly have been a teacher if he had taken term-time holidays. Maybe he had still been a student? That would make him younger than her. She flicked to the first page to check his date of birth, but her gaze snagged on the photo. Most people had horrid passport photos, but Brad Wilson's wouldn't have looked out of place in a modeling agency's catalogue. Then she checked his date of birth. No, he wasn't younger than her. In fact, he was two years older.

The door opened suddenly and she clapped the passport shut and shoved it under a pile of books, as if it were a porn magazine.

It was Mildred from the science department. "Sonia, I've already asked Brad, but I thought that I should ask you too, since you're the trip leader. Could you bring back some rock samples from Etna for our geology collection?"

"Sure."

"Thank you. Have fun! I'm sure you will."

Did she detect a hint of an innuendo in Mildred's words or was she becoming paranoid? It was perfectly possible to go on a school trip with a hunky colleague without having a crush on him—or developing one.

As soon as Mildred was gone, Sonia snapped a photo of the first page of the passport and emailed it to the travel agent. Now she could rid herself of the document. Brad had told Chantelle to put it in his pigeonhole, but Sonia didn't like leaving such an important document on a shelf in the staffroom. If it went missing, Brad wouldn't have enough time to get a replacement before the trip. She should have asked Mildred to take it back to him. *Too late now.*

Reluctantly, she picked it up, plodded to the science block and stopped outside the science office. If another teacher answered the door, she'd give them the document and ask them to pass it on to him. But what if *he* answered? Would she just hand him the passport or would she be obliged to start a conversation? They were going to be a team in charge of twenty-eight children for a week, so they should try and make a chink in the ice—or at least just thaw it a little. It wouldn't be fair if the children suffered because of their friction. She smoothed her dress, drew a breath and knocked.

"Come in." His gravelly voice set her heart racing. She was a grown-up, for goodness' sake. She shouldn't be afraid of another teacher, even an extremely surly one. She opened the door and stepped inside. As he registered her presence, his features immediately tightened, and he got up from behind his desk.

"Thanks for the passport. I gave the travel agent what they needed and I don't need it anymore." She thrust the document at him.

"Good." He strode toward her but, as became obvious a moment later, it wasn't so much out of courtesy as to prevent her from advancing farther into the room. There was no trace of the smiles he had regaled the kids with earlier.

His eagerness to take the passport matched her keenness to give it back and they overshot, causing their fingers to touch. It lasted a millisecond, because he immediately retracted his hand, wincing, as if he'd been stung.

"Do you need anything else from me?" he asked curtly.

Sonia's ice-breaking resolution wobbled like a clown on a tightrope. To make a chink in his glacier, she would need a pickaxe and a flamethrower. But she was determined to try. "I understand that Mildred has asked you to collect rock samples from Etna. Would you like to know which other places we'll be visiting?"

"Not really." He shifted closer to the door and opened it for her, as if waiting for her to leave.

Can he really be that rude?

He must have noticed her shock, because he rushed to add, "I'm sorry, but I'm really busy right now." His expression had softened a little, but he didn't let go of the door.

Just then, Mildred peeped in. "Hi, Brad. I see on the timetable that you have a free period now. Could we look at the KS3 curriculum?"

Really busy right now?

Mildred noticed Sonia. "Oh. Sorry to interrupt."

"No worries. I was just going."

Unsurprisingly, Brad didn't try to stop her from leaving. As she walked back to the languages block, Sonia reflected on the Italian proverb, *meglio soli che male accompagnati—better alone than in bad company*. She would much rather have been the awkward third person on Jack and Katie's honeymoon than have Brad come too.

That evening, as she packed her bags, Sonia gazed at the cloudy sky outside the window of her flat. There wouldn't be many clouds in Sicily, if she remembered right. The last time she had been there had been just before her life had disintegrated. She hadn't been able to face going back since. Anything to do with her parents' birthplace reminded her of their prejudices, patriarchy and false sense of honor. Would they have been more understanding, more forgiving, more open-minded about her life if they hadn't grown up in Palermo? For years, she had found it less hurtful to pin the blame on their Sicilian upbringing rather than on them as people. But now Sonia wanted to make peace with the land whose colors she bore on her skin.

There was no way she would ever go back to Sicily with her parents. She hardly saw them these days, anyway. But going with her students, her children, was her best chance to get over her issues. Every British person she knew who had visited Sicily had fallen in love with it. There must be more to the island than intruding relatives, bigotry and stifling traditions. Going with her students, she might be able to look at her ancestral land with forgiving eyes and finally be able to feel proud of it.

Her gaping suitcase beckoned one last check. Sun lotion, tick. *Goggles, tick. Swimmers, tick.* By refusing to listen to any of her plans for the trip, Brad had no idea that they would be swimming. She would have a clandestine giggle when he turned up at the beach without swimming trunks. *Deodorant, tick. Travel sickness tabs, tick. Asthma inhaler, tick.* She paused, toying with the zipper on her travel case. Stress made her asthma worse, and this was no time to be taking chances. She went to her drawer, picked up and popped in a second inhaler.

Chapter Two

The coach was there, Jake and Katie were already nesting inside and the students were swarming around the car park, but there was no sign of Brad Wilson. Was he going to pull a no-show? Sonia rummaged in her handbag, checking for her blue inhalers.

"Miss Alletti, hello. Could I have a word with you?" Charlotte Rogers' mum greeted her in a whisper, darting glances at her daughter and her friends, probably to make sure that they were out of earshot.

"Sure."

"I don't know if Charlotte has told you," she said quietly, "but her father and I are going through a difficult patch."

"I had a feeling that might be the case," she replied.

"Things are tough at home and I'm worried about Charlotte. The other day I caught her watching a teen suicide video." The woman's voice broke and her eyes glistened with repressed tears. "Please, will you keep an eye on her? She's my only child and God only knows what I went through to have her."

24

Her last words beckoned unwelcome memories and Sonia tensed. "I will," she said, keeping her voice gentle.

But the woman pressed on. "Will you look after her as if she were your own daughter?"

This conversation was beginning to hit too close to home. Charlotte *could* have been her daughter. She *could* have been the mother of a girl Charlotte's age. Her daughter would have turned twelve the past January if... She shuddered. *Don't think about it.* "I will. I promise."

"Seeing her watching those videos, Miss Alletti... You can imagine how I felt."

Sonia's chest squeezed. No, she couldn't imagine. She didn't have the right to, not after she had been the one to... *Don't think about it.*

Charlotte's mum pulled a well-used tissue out of her pocket and wiped her eyes. Sonia stroked her arm, even though she felt like crying too. "I'll watch over Charlotte as if she were my own. Don't worry."

"Thank you." The woman gave Sonia a smile brimming with gratitude.

Leaving, the mother walked up to her daughter, probably hoping for a goodbye kiss, but Charlotte waved her off and turned her back before her mum could get close enough for any physical contact. With her shoulders curled like an autumn leaf, the woman trudged back to her car. Sonia couldn't have felt sorrier for her.

Just then, a sports car slipped into the parking space next to the woman's car. The door opened and Brad Wilson emerged in all his arrogant glory. Even in a loose pair of jeans and a dark blue T-shirt, the guy looked like he'd stepped out of a fashion catalogue. Unfairly, being one hundred per cent rude didn't seem to stop him from possessing a natural elegance. He swaggered toward the group, in no apparent hurry to join them, although they were about to embark on a week-long trip together. He acknowledged Sonia with a cursory nod, much the same as when they crossed paths in the corridor. Sonia reciprocated with just-as-reluctant a nod.

Breathe. Relax. Don't let him get under your skin. Don't let him spoil the trip.

"Right. We can go now." As Sonia called their names from the register, the children filed into the coach, filling it from the back. Only when she and Brad were left outside did he gesture for her to climb in first. She chose one of the few double seats left, resigned to spending three hours sitting next to Brad. She had prepared a battle plan—or at least a few neutral subjects to talk about. She would brief him about the activities for the trip, for a start. If he was going to be of any help, he would need to know what was going on. That would make a nice and neutral topic of conversation.

But, instead of taking the empty seat next to hers, he plonked himself in another row, on the other side of the corridor, plugged in his earphones and stared out of the window.

Well, all right. The guy was clearly uninterested in them getting to know each other. But wasn't he even a little curious to know where they were going, what they would see? A suspicion sneaked into Sonia's mind. Maybe he didn't care about the schedule because he wasn't intending to get involved. After all, it was his presence, not his active participation, that was necessary for the trip to go ahead.

She felt her skin spike with irritation. It wasn't that she needed his help, as Mrs. Ashcroft had said. She would have happily taken all twenty-eight kids on her own. But the thought that he intended to enjoy a holiday on the school's dime without lifting a finger in return made Sonia's blood turn to lava.

All through the trip, she kept darting stormy glances in his direction, even though all he could see of him was a cheekbone that was perfectly shaped, a mop of hair that was sexily disheveled and a shoulder that was wide and sturdy-looking. Now that this trip had forced her to pay attention to Brad Wilson, she had to admit that the guy was undeniably handsome. But good looks didn't justify laziness, not in *her* world. She would jolly well make sure that Brad Wilson would earn his keep.

As soon as their coach swung into Gatwick Airport, she leaped out of her seat and flung her clipboard onto his lap. "You'll take the register while I check out how to walk to Departures." She walked up to the front of the coach so that he couldn't easily give back the clipboard. The moment the coach stopped, she was out.

There was no real need for the recce. The way to Departures was obvious. Still, she wanted to send Brad a clear signal. *You will share the work.* With Jake and Katie it was different. Jake wasn't teaching staff and he was paid hourly, term-time only. Katie didn't even work for the school. But Brad was a teacher with a full salary and extra on top for being a head of a department.

Sonia marched into the Departures hall, checked which entrance was closer to their check-in desk then made her way back. As she got closer to the coach, a confident male voice speaking in Italian wafted out of the vehicle. Was the driver Italian and she hadn't realized it? She climbed the steps and found that the voice didn't belong to the driver. It was Brad's.

"You said that you didn't speak Italian," she accused him.

"Mr. Wilson has just learned it. He's learned it on the coach!" the kids told her excitedly.

Grinning, he tilted his phone to show her a language learning podcast. *No way.* He must have studied Italian before. He must have been pulling the children's legs and undermining the whole of language teaching in the process. She forced out a sarcastic smile. "Well done to you, clever Mr. Wilson."

He crinkled his face into the loveliest smile, even better than the one he had given the children when he'd burst into Sonia's class. Did he think that she was paying him a sincere compliment? Sonia felt a little rush of guilt.

If Brad Wilson was achingly handsome when he scowled, he was knee-crumplingly gorgeous when he smiled. But it wasn't just the crinkles and dimples of that smile that startled Sonia. It was also the fact that the smile was…directed at her!

"*Complimenti. I tuoi bambini sono bravissimi,*" he replied in a voice that was even huskier in Italian than it was in English. He was *congratulating her* for *her* children's Italian. Sonia had to hold on to the headrest of the nearest seat.

"*Grazie,*" she managed to squeeze out of the place in her throat where her breath had caught. She couldn't fail to notice that, as well as paying her a compliment, he had also addressed her with the Italian friendly form of '*tu*' instead of the formal '*lei*'. Was it just a beginner's mistake or a sign that he was stepping down from his ivory tower? Sonia did a double-take at the language learning podcast still glowing on his phone's screen. If that app could improve character that much, as well as language skills, she must try it too.

* * * *

He should have used the formal *'lei'*. He had no excuses. He knew about it because he had studied it in the podcast. He should have kept his distance, at least verbally, given that there was nothing he could do about their physical proximity. The plane seats allocated to them were 12B and 12C. He had offered to sit with the kids to keep a better eye on them, but the fierce air hostess had insisted that everyone must sit in the seat printed on their boarding pass. Now he was forced to brush elbows and knees with Sonia, feel the warmth of her body next to his. Her purple flower-print dress reminded him of berry pies, summer nights and the lavender blossoms that fill the air with their scent. *Her scent*. On the return flight, he absolutely *must* find a way to avoid sitting next to her. The craft started taxiing. It was too late to run away.

"Have you been to Sicily before?" she asked him.

Oh God, even her voice turns me on. It was modulated like music, deep and sexy. "Never," he said curtly.

"Do you travel much?" she continued, popping a piece of chewing gum in her mouth.

"A fair bit."

"Where have you been?"

Brad was tempted to abort the conversation once and for all with a 'here and there', but something stopped him. What would she think of him if he brushed her off like that? She must have already formed a pretty low opinion of him after months of him giving her the cold shoulder. He had seen her go from the initial hurt of the first few times to the latest flint-faced hostility — and he hadn't liked it. If he carried on snubbing her, she'd shut even the last door on him — assuming that it wasn't locked and barred already.

What she thought of him on a personal level shouldn't—and didn't—matter to him, of course. In fact, it was better to keep their relationship as cold and distant as possible. But, unfortunately, they were on this trip together, and even the most basic functional work-relationship, especially given these circumstances, required a little more closeness than they'd had until now. "My latest trip was to Uganda last summer."

She thought about it for a moment then seemed satisfied. "A safari, right?"

He snorted a laugh. "Not exactly. Only if you call performing surgery in a refugee camp a safari."

Her eyes widened and she stopped chewing her gum. "Surgery?"

In two beats they had got from a harmless question about holidays to a full disclosure of his life. He squirmed, but it was too late to go back on it. "Yes. I was a surgeon before becoming a teacher."

"Wow. People told me that you had medical training, but I didn't—"

"Who told you that? What did they tell you?" he snapped, more harshly than he'd meant to. If his medical past was known in the school, chances were that the reasons he'd left that world behind were also the subject of gossip. Memories of the motorbike accident flooded back. The despair and the guilt at discovering that Frances was dead while he had survived, his decision to abandon his surgical career, the disapproval of his family and friends...

Everyone had advised him to take time off, to wait till the wounds had healed—both the physical ones and the others—before making important decisions, but he hadn't. While everything else had been thick fog, one certainty had beamed like a beacon. He would never again accept payment for saving people's lives, not after he had ended the one life that had mattered most to him. With his medical background, retraining as a biology teacher had been simple. Teaching kids was now his penance, his way of paying back some of his debt for being alive. During the school holidays he continued to volunteer with Doctors Without Borders, as he had done ever since becoming a medical student. Each time he helped a student with a difficult biology topic or with the pains of growing up, each time he removed a piece of shrapnel from someone's body, each time he saved someone's limb, he felt like he had made a chip in his debt. But it was never entirely paid back. It would never be.

"Chantelle told me that you had medical training. That's all," Sonia said defensively, shifting a little away from him.

"People should mind their own business."

The airplane's engines revved, acceleration pressing his already-tight chest against the seat. He noticed Sonia grip the armrest, while the packet of travel sickness gum rested on her dress in the lovely dip between her legs. For a moment, he wished his hand was that packet, but he chased the thought away. Her olive skin had turned ashen and her lips were now a shade of lavender. She was either travel sick or scared. "Are you all right?"

"People should mind their own business, shouldn't they?" she snapped.

"*Touché.*" He pressed his shoulders against the seat's back.

"I'm sorry, Brad. I don't travel well," she said in a softer tone. She had never used that tone with him — nor pronounced his name like that. Instantly something melted in his chest.

She pulled an asthma inhaler out of her bag, shook it hard and squeezed a puff into her mouth. Brad felt his own lungs squeeze tight. *She suffers from asthma.* Was she going to be all right?

"Could you check that the kids are okay? If I turn my head, I'll be sick," she said matter-of-factly.

The kids in the rows behind them were busy looking out of the windows or playing on their phones. "Everyone is fine except you. Let me make you better," he heard himself say.

Her eyebrows shot to her hairline but that didn't stop him. He gently wrapped her wrist in his hand. At his touch, her tendons tensed and a little jerk suggested that her first reaction had been to pull away but she had resisted it. He glanced at her to make sure that he could proceed. She averted her gaze but relaxed her arm and offered him the other one too. He took it as a permission.

Gently running his thumbs over the soft insides of her wrists, he found the pressure points he needed and started massaging them. Her skin felt smooth and firm, as olive-like in texture as it was in hue. The last bit of tension drained out of her and she closed her eyes, surrendering. Color slowly returned to her cheeks and lips but Brad couldn't tell whether it was the nausea leaving her or whether she was blushing.

He was well used to handling people's bodies, but still, at the contact of her skin, all his sensory neurons fired at once. Heck, the massage was affecting the masseur more than the recipient. Brad had started to feel totally out of his depth when the aircraft jerked and lifted off into the air.

It couldn't have just been the acupressure that was making her whole body tingle with pleasure. The moment she'd felt his hand on her skin, a frisson of pure electricity had whizzed up her arm. His touch had sent her aerophobia spinning out of her head and turned her brain into soft, sweet candy floss. Being inside a metal tube hurtling through the sky didn't frighten her anymore. Her head was in the clouds already. If she felt like that when only her wrists were wrapped in his hands, how would she feel if her entire body was enveloped in his arms?

Don't even think about it.

This wasn't supposed to happen. She had sworn to herself that she would not fall for a man ever again — emotionally, mentally or even just physically. The last time she had gotten too close to someone, terrible things had happened. And this particular specimen was sewn together with red flags — cocky, surly *and* handsome. *Triple trouble.* She was playing with fire, a whole bonfire of it, but the warmth it emanated was irresistible. Plus, his massage was helping her travel sickness more than any pill or gum had ever done before. Did it matter whether it was to do with pressure points or with her longing to nestle into his chest? That body-melting smile he had given her on the coach had shifted something inside her. A switch had been flicked and now it was stuck in the 'on' position. Instead of pulling her wrists away, she closed her eyes and let pleasure flood her body.

She had been unfair to him. She had imagined him enjoying exclusive winter-sun safaris when, in fact, he had been slaving away in refugee camps. She connected her mind with the entry and exit date stamps in his passports. He had been to Haiti right after that terrible earthquake and to Sierra Leone during the Ebola outbreak.

She had asked him about his travels only to test his sincerity. She'd intended to crosscheck his answers against the visa stamps on his passport, which she remembered, to see if he would tell her the truth. She hadn't expected to slash into his past and open a Chinese box of questions. Why would he leave a well-paid medical career for a teaching job after years of studying and specialist training? She was dying to ask, but his reaction to her mention of the rumors about him made her think better of it. The first thing she'd do when she got back to school would be to ask Chantelle for more information. Unless, of course, by the end of the trip, they'd grown so close that she could ask him directly.

Now that's a dangerous thought.

"Righto. I'm sure you're all better now." He dropped her wrists as if they had burned his fingers.

The cold shock of the armrest after the warmth of his hands jolted Sonia out of her reverie. She flipped her eyes open and she saw him yank the inflight magazine out of the seat pocket and open it to a random page. *What the heck?* How could the reviews of Lisbon's diners be so suddenly and urgently interesting? She checked her wrists for anything that might have offended him. *Nothing.* She mentally added another item to the list of his dangerous attributes...*mercurial.*

The seatbelt sign went off and she got up, allegedly to check on the kids but really to get away from him.

The girls on the last row were giggly and noisy. "Miss, my can exploded," Charlotte Rogers announced, her jeans and blouse drenched in Coca-Cola.

"She shook it, Miss," her friends accused her.

Sonia walked up to them, sighing internally. "How did you even get this can?"

"I bought it at the gate, just before they called us for boarding."

"Have you got spare clothes in your hand luggage?"

"I don't know. My mum packed it."

Sonia rolled her eyes and opened the overhead lockers. "Which one is yours?"

"The turquoise one."

Thankfully the turquoise trolley was close enough to the edge to spare her the indignity of clambering onto the seat. She reached up and pulled it down.

The girl rummaged inside without any care for the neatly folded clothes. "Oh, no. She's packed stuff that hasn't fit me for years."

"Why didn't you pack your own bags?"

Charlotte ignored her question and replied simply, "I don't need any clothes. I'll dry out," the girl scoffed through her chattering teeth. The aircraft's climate control was fiercely cold and she was already a little blue.

Please, look after her as if she was your own daughter, her mother had told Sonia. "No way. If you catch a chill, one of the adults will have to stay back in the hotel to look after you." Sonia wriggled out of her own cardigan and handed it to her. "Go to the toilet and change into this. I'll get you a pair of jeans in a moment." The girl got up and did as she'd been told, while Sonia returned to her seat.

Brad darted a furtive glance at her over the top of his magazine, followed by a double-take, which immediately made her self-conscious about her spaghetti-strapped dress.

"Charlotte Rogers has spilled her drink and she's freezing. I had to give her my cardigan," she explained, reaching up for the overhead locker.

Brad sprang to his feet. "Let me get it for you. You're cold, *piccina*."

His words and his tone knocked Sonia off balance. Only a few minutes before he had dropped her wrists as if they were scorpions and now he was calling her *piccina*, 'little', as if she were his baby. She stood frozen to the spot while he reached up into the locker.

"Which one is yours?" he asked her, catching her just when her eyes had wandered to a flash of torso temporarily exposed by his rising T-shirt. It was lean and toned, with just the right amount of hair in the right places.

"Ahem…the purple one," she said.

"I should have guessed."

Was it a compliment?

He pulled her case out of the locker as if it weren't any heavier than a magazine and lowered it onto their seats.

She thanked him and had just opened the case, exposing the rambunctious mess inside it, when a woman's voice rang out above her shoulders. "Excuse me?" The air hostess was pointing the drinks trolley at her like a battering ram about to strike.

Brad moved out of the way and retreated to his seat, but he couldn't sit down, so he stayed standing in the gap. There was nowhere for Sonia to go other than to squeeze into that gap with him. Reluctantly, she reversed into the tiny space. The hostess pushed forward a little and darted her an impatient glance. Sonia was still in the way. She inched back until her backside was pressed against Brad's leg. She felt its firmness and warmth. His scent enveloped her and desire whooshed through her, flushing her cheeks and sending her heartbeat haywire. She ached to turn around and… What?

Quick, trolley, go!

It took the trolley a few interminable seconds to maneuver past them and, as soon as it had pulled through, Sonia and Brad popped out of their space like corks out of a bottle. Avoiding his gaze, Sonia hastily pulled her jeans out of the suitcase, stuffed the panties and bras back in and hastened to zip it all up as if she were trying to stuff all the world's evil back into Pandora's box. Just as urgently, Brad lifted the case back up into the locker and returned to his seat, where he plugged in his earphones and resumed his magazine reading—still on the same page. He looked just as awkward as Sonia felt, and she hoped he hadn't seen her blush. A few minutes later, the hostess was back, offering drinks. Brad asked for water, with plenty of ice.

As soon as Sonia had left to go give her jeans to Charlotte Rogers, Brad reached up to his hand luggage and pulled out a green cashmere jumper. The sight of her naked shoulders had been too much to bear, even before she had pressed herself against his leg. It had taken a superhuman effort not to wrap his arms around her and kiss the delicate curve of her neck, where a few rebellious curls swung from her messy bun. He couldn't understand how such a minute woman could turn him into a horny teenager at thirty. There was something about her—in every way—something he couldn't put his finger on that pressed all his buttons.

"All good. My jeans fit Charlotte," she announced cheerily, returning from her mission. She plonked herself back into her seat. Her lovely shoulders were still exposed.

"I'm not surprised." She was as petite as a twelve-year-old. And there was another contradiction. Despite her size, she managed to control her students with the authority of a giant. Her slender neck produced a voice powerful enough to fill corridors. He'd heard how she had fought for the grants that had made this whole trip possible. Other teachers said that she was a force to be reckoned with, and he was getting a taste of that, albeit in a different department. It was a force that he urgently needed to snuff under a jumper. "You'll be cold. Take this."

"No, thanks. I'm fine."

"I don't need it. You can have it," he insisted.

"Really, I'm fine." She politely pushed the jumper away.

"You'll be cold."

She tensed up. "I think that I'm old enough to look after my own temperature."

Oh, no. She thought that he was patronizing her. He certainly couldn't tell her that he needed her to cover up her décolleté because, from his position, he could see more than a man strapped to a seat should see. And that glimpse of a lacy navy-blue bra made him wish he could see more. "Just do it," he rasped.

She crossed her arms defiantly. Unfortunately, this had the side effect of pushing her breasts up and pulling her dress down, exposing her even more. He groaned inwardly. This trip was going to be even more difficult than he had expected. He had agreed to it in the hope of giving the children an educational experience and memories to treasure. Now he just hoped to get through the trip without doing anything that he would regret. The regret compartments in his brain and heart were already full to overflowing. "As you wish." He laid the jumper in his lap, picked up the magazine again and flicked the pages to the aircraft specifications section. That should take his mind off lacy blue bras.

The hostesses returned with their trolley, this time full of watches, jewelry and perfumes. An annoyingly loud voice guaranteed that they were absolute bargains. Brad wondered if Sonia wore any perfume or if she just smelled lovely naturally. A baby started crying and, almost immediately after, the pilot announced that they had started their descent and would soon be landing at Palermo's Falcone Borsellino Airport. The sun was gliding under the horizon, painting the clouds with strokes of blush and lilac. The sea below sparkled and glittered, and jagged mountains shot above the coastline where the city and the villages twinkled like fairy lights.

The reverse thrust roared as the airplane slowed for landing. Sonia's knuckles went white on the armrest again, but Brad didn't dare do anything about it. They touched the ground with a little bump and she gave a little sigh. Even that sound was enough to turn him on. If this was the way things were between them, he had a feeling that his troubles might have only just begun.

Chapter Three

Sonia had been tempted to accept his jumper, just because she was already freezing, but she hadn't liked the way he was pushing it on her. It reminded her too much of her mother forcing some itchy woolen home-knitted cardigans on her as a child, with the promise that they would stave off every illness from simple colds to the bubonic plague. In any case, it was a poisoned gift, bound to be full of his scent. The way his proximity and touch played havoc on her senses unsettled her. What was it about Brad Wilson that made her kneecaps wobble when he smiled at her and her skin break into goosebumps when he touched her wrists? He had never flirted with her — in fact, quite the opposite. The guy had made it abundantly clear that he wasn't a fan. Yes, he was very attractive, but she was immune to men now — attractive ones especially.

Whatever it was about Brad Wilson, she had to put a stop to it before it got out of control. She didn't do 'out of control' anymore. It wasn't just because of the mess and heartache that came with men but also because he was a colleague. Her job was her life and her future, and it was to protect her life and her future that she had suppressed another life, back in those horrible days when she had been sixteen. If she hadn't let her own child get in the way of her future, she certainly wouldn't let Brad Wilson.

Out of the window she saw the sapphire sea glitter, and out of the blue—literally—she felt the airplane bump in to land.

Managing the excited children off the plane, through immigration and onto the coach kept her mind off unholy thoughts. On the coach to the hotel, everyone managed to sit in the same places they had sat on the other coach. Disappointment pricked at her when she saw Brad lag behind and board last to make sure he could sit on his own. She acknowledged that she should keep her distance from him, but it still stung. Pride told her that keeping apart should be her doing, not his. By the time they arrived at their hotel, it had gone dark and everyone was tired and hungry. Unfortunately, the reception was bustling with new arrivals and there was a queue to check in.

"What are we waiting for?" one of the kids whined.

"Our turn to check in," Brad answered calmly.

"But I'm hungry," another protested.

"The staff won't understand you unless you say *ho fame*," Brad said.

"Did you really learn Italian on the coach, Mr. Wilson?" a child asked.

"Of course. I never lie."

"Mr. Wilson never lies!" the child shouted.

A variant of the good old Truth or Dare game ensued, which Sonia was grateful for as a distraction for the hungry children. She also found it quite entertaining. The children shamelessly asked Brad everything from how often he shaved to whether he had ever eaten his own boogie. He admitted that he had. There were things she too would have liked to ask him—about his past as a surgeon, for example—but they were not for that company. So, she just enjoyed watching the game until the questions started to become a little too personal for comfort.

"Are you married, Mr. Wilson?" one of the girls asked.

"No, I'm not."

"Have you got a girlfriend?"

"No."

At that answer, much to her shock, her heart did a little somersault. But then she heard something that set off her internal nuclear Armageddon sirens. Charlotte whispered to Laura, "Ask him if he has a crush on Miss Alletti."

Under no circumstance should she let that question be asked. "Right, kids," she piped up in a clarion voice, "let's leave Mr. Wilson with Mr. and Mrs. Jenkins to queue for us while we check out tonight's menu."

Much to Sonia's relief, all the kids followed her to the restaurant's board and the game was dropped. On the way back, the kids discovered the games area and happily stopped at the table football and snooker tables while Sonia perched herself on a bar stool from where she could simultaneously keep an eye on them and on Brad's progress at the queue. It was lovely seeing the kids enjoy themselves as they played. Table football and snooker were much more wholesome than Truth or Dare. Thank goodness she had stopped it before it was too late. Whatever had got into Charlotte's head?

Hold on. Where was the girl? Her friends were huddled by the vending machines, but she wasn't with them. She wasn't at the snooker table or the table football or the candy grabber. Sonia wriggled off the bar stool and started asking around. No one had seen Charlotte since they'd left the check-in queue. Her pulse rising, Sonia looked in the ladies' room. No luck. She rushed to check the bench by the entrance, peered down the approach road that wriggled up the hill then searched the front garden. No sign of Charlotte. Cold sweat started to bead on her forehead. If she didn't find Charlotte in the back garden, she would have to raise an alarm. Sonia ran back in and burst through the double doors that opened to the back. A heady scent of citrus blossom hit her and she saw a small figure huddled on a bench overlooking a luxuriant lemon orchard.

Phew, I found her.

Sonia waited for her breathing to steady itself. She didn't want Charlotte to know that she had been so worried. Then she walked down to the bench and sat.

"Lovely view, isn't it?" she said as nonchalantly as she could.

"How did you know I was here, Miss?" the girl asked, with her gaze fixed on the sunset.

"I like to keep an eye on my clothes."

Charlotte darted a quick glance at the jeans and the red cardigan she was wearing, before the edges of her mouth curled into the inkling of a smile. "Your clothes are comfy. I think that I would like to be you, Miss."

That was an unusually personal comment—and a flattering one too. Sonia felt a tingle of pride.

"You always look happy, Miss. I can't imagine you sad."

"I can assure you that I get my sad moments too, from time to time. And I got a lot more of them when I was your age."

"I hate being my age. I hate being me."

"It's hard when your parents are having trouble —"

"That's only half the problem, Miss."

Sonia waited for Charlotte to say more, if she wanted to.

"My dad didn't want me. He wanted my mum to have an abortion."

Sonia shuddered. The word 'abortion' was like a skein of barbed wire for her.

"Mum refused and, every time they fight, he brings it up. I should have never been born. If I didn't exist, they wouldn't be arguing."

Sonia insides wrenched. If she had given up her studies and kept her baby girl, would her daughter be happy? Would she blame herself for her mum's lack of job opportunities? Asking questions like these was like hopping on broken glass in bare feet.

A light breeze made the dark citrus fronds quiver and ripple like the surface of a lake. "You will never know how your parents' life would have been without you. Even if they were still together and your dad was happier, your mum might have been much sadder. I have a feeling that she would have rather keep you and lose your dad than have your dad and lose you."

Charlotte whipped round to face her. "What makes you think that?"

Sonia swallowed to steady her voice. "In the car park before we left, your mum asked me to keep a special eye on you during this trip. She made me promise to look after you as if you were my own daughter."

Charlotte's eyes glistened with tears.

"I admire your mum. She had the guts to keep you, even though it might cost her the marriage. Not everyone is so brave. Please, be kind to her."

Just then, someone called from the double doors. "Miss, Miss! Mr. Wilson is looking for you."

Brad seemed to be having an animated discussion with the receptionist.

"Is everything all right?" Sonia asked, walking up to them.

"Did you book fifteen twins and a double?" Brad asked.

The receptionist's Ferrari-red fingernails clacked frantically against a screen. "That's what I've got on the system."

"Yes. The double is for Jake and Katie," Sonia replied calmly.

Brad looked increasingly agitated. "But we need one double, fourteen twins and *two singles*."

Oh. My. God. "I'm really sorry. I know what happened. I was going to share a twin with Kate but I forgot to change the booking when she couldn't come anymore." Her eyes darted between Brad and the receptionist, pleading forgiveness from one and help from the other. "I'm really sorry. It's entirely my mistake. Can we turn one of the twins into two singles?"

The woman puckered her lips, which were the same hue as her fingernails, and shot Sonia a knowing look. Did she think that Sonia had meant to 'forget' to change the booking? *Oh, please!* Did Brad think that too? Sonia's cheeks went into spontaneous combustion.

The receptionist tapped and swiped, swiped and tapped, shaking her head and pursing her penciled-rimmed lips. "It's the Festival of the Blood Orange. We're quite full."

Sonia's stomach sank to her knees and Brad's facial expression suggested that he too might be suffering a similar rearrangement of internal body organs.

"Please." Sonia's voice was halfway between a bleat and a whimper.

After more tapping, headshaking and lip-puckering, the woman fluttered her plastic lashes and declared, "I'm sorry. We've got no singles left."

"Then we'll have another twin—or anything else you've got." The desperation in Brad's voice was a little hurtful.

"All I can give you is one of the VIP suites, but I'll have to charge you the full pr—."

"That's absolutely fine," Brad interrupted, reaching into his pocket.

"I'll get this. It's been my fault." Sonia laid her hand on his arm to stop him and he flinched. *Great.*

"No." He flapped her away as if she were an annoying insect.

"I insist."

"And I don't care." He whipped his credit card out and slid it across the desk.

The receptionist took it.

Sonia didn't know how to react. Should she thank him for what was actually a very kind gesture or should she be cross about the manner of the delivery? Perhaps he was so insistent on paying because he wanted the suite for himself. Judging by the price, it must be a very fine accommodation. Maybe he was just desperate to get out of sharing the twin with her. *That* desperate? Did he worry that she would try to have it on with him the moment he closed the door? *As if!*

"Actually"—the receptionist peered into the screen as if it was a crystal ball—"we don't have any doubles left either. I'll have to give you another VIP suite instead of the double that you've booked, but I won't charge you the difference for this one."

Well, wasn't that a nice silver lining for their cumulonimbus? Jake and Katie would surely be pleased.

"So that's two suites and fifteen twins." The lady slid a bunch of key cards across the counter in Brad's direction. "One last thing… The VIP suites are only for adults. Under-sixteens are strictly not allowed. These yellow key cards are for the twins, which are all on the third floor. These pink key cards are for the suites. They're on the top floor."

Ah! Brad's offer to foot the suite's bill made sense now. From his extensive experience of traveling, he must have known that the VIP suite was likely to be on a different floor from the kids' twins. If he took it, he wouldn't be the first port of call for night-time dramas.

"Thanks." Brad caught the bunch and diverted one of the pink cards to Sonia. "That's for you."

There she was, thinking that he was a free-rider, when he was actually extremely, utterly kind. He had footed the bill for her mishap, given her the best room and taken her off night duty. "Thanks," she mumbled. But it didn't seem like enough.

* * * *

Brad chose the twin for himself that was right in the middle of the boys' corridor so that they wouldn't be able to sneak into each other's rooms without having to tiptoe past his door. With Sonia sleeping on a different floor, he'd be the adult on night-duty. Two by two, he started delivering the boys to their accommodations with instructions to be ready for dinner in fifteen minutes.

He had gotten to the last room when, as he opened the door, a wall of cold air tumbled onto him as if he'd stepped into an industrial fridge. Dust blanketed every surface and a stale musty smell lingered in the air. The heating control panel was dead. Everything suggested that this room hadn't been used for some time. He picked up the phone and dialed the concierge.

"Hallo?"

Brad recognized the voice of the lady who had served them earlier. She had a petite, slender figure and long dark hair in a ponytail. In many ways, she looked similar to Sonia and yet she was incredibly different. It wasn't just the way Sonia moved, spoke or dressed that set her apart. He couldn't quite tell what it was, but the difference between the two of them was like that between the sun and a desk lamp. "Hello, this is Mr. Wilson. We have a problem with the heating in room three-o-five."

"All right... I'll send someone up as soon as possible."

"Thanks." Then he led the boys downstairs for dinner.

Jake and Katie were sitting at a table for two, staring into each other's eyes like two blinkered horses. Damien flicked a tiny projectile—a clump of bread? A crumb of grissini?—across to their table and it landed in one of their wineglasses with a little splash, but neither Jake nor Katie noticed and Brad decided it was best not to tell them.

Sonia and the girls were sitting at a table long enough to accommodate everyone. She was staring pensively out of the window, languidly beautiful, and Brad let his gaze linger on her. What was she thinking about? Or...who? Much to his shock, the thought of a man in Sonia's life filled him with jealousy. To shake these thoughts out of his head—or hers?—he asked her about the rooms.

"The girls' are fine. I haven't checked mine yet. I was in a hurry to come down and make sure that there were no surprises with the dinner. They've assured me that our meals are on their way, but we'll have to wait because they're very busy." She placed a hand over the nape of her neck and threw her head backward to stretch. Even that simple gesture had a swan-like elegance, strong and delicate at the same time. But she looked very tired, and he ached to wrap her in his arms and let her rest her head on his chest.

Get away from her.

"In that case, I'll take the kids outside for some games," he offered, glancing at some of the boys who had started building a tower with the drinking glasses.

"Thank you, Brad. You're a star," she said.

Was it the compliment or just the sound of his name on her lips that gave him a certain lightness in the pit of his stomach? *It's just hunger.* "Right, kids. Who wants to go out and play in the garden?"

"Me!" most of the children shouted.

Feeling a little like the Pied Piper of Hamelin, he led the little crowd outside. Out there, the stars looked like diamonds mounted in a vault of onyx and the air smelled of citrus blossoms. He wished Sonia could see and smell that too. *Stop thinking about her!* He must keep his mind's eyes firmly fixed on the reason he was there—to give the kids a learning opportunity and a holiday to remember.

After a few rounds of night tag—a new version of tag that he had just invented—they were finally called for dinner. The kids rushed to choose their seats, leaving him no choice but to sit next to Sonia.

It's still better than sharing a bedroom.

A fragrant plate of pasta with homemade tomato sauce was put before him and he was just about to tuck into it with gusto when he spotted the concierge tottering across the dining room toward him. The apologetic frown etched on her face filled him with an unpleasant sense of foreboding.

"Mr. Wilson, I'm really sorry, but the heating in room three-o-five cannot be repaired tonight. We've called the technician, but he can't come until Monday. I'm afraid we haven't got any other room to give you for tonight—"

"Never mind. I'll be all right." Thanks to the mishap, his room was also a twin. He could take the cold. He had been through much worse in the course of his overseas volunteering.

The woman pursed her shockingly red lips and shook her ponytail. "I'm sorry, but it's against the law for us to give you a room that cold."

Since when had Italians cared about legality? "Look… I really don't mind. I promise that I'm not going to sue you," he snapped. *Relax, Brad.*

"I'm really sorry but, if I let you have that room, I'll get into trouble with the bosses."

Brad ran a hand over his face and inwardly cursed the moment he had picked up the phone to report the fault. "All right, then what solution do you suggest? Can we put an extra bed into another room?"

The woman scrunched her face. It was probably meant to look cutely apologetic but it didn't. "We have a lot of families staying tonight and all the extra beds are in use."

Sonia was answering the kids' questions about horrific Sicilian earthquakes, so she was totally oblivious to the unfolding drama. The concierge's eyes kept swiveling in Sonia's direction until Brad got the hint.

"I'm not sharing a room with my *colleague*," he said, with an emphasis on 'colleague', just to make things clear.

As if she'd been called by name, Sonia whipped her head around. "Are you talking about me?"

Her candid smile made Brad feel a little guilty about his refusal. *Why should I feel guilty? I shouldn't be obliged to share with her.* "The heating in one of the twins is faulty and it won't be repaired until Monday. The hotel won't let me have the room, even though I assured them that I don't mind. But they have no other rooms to give us."

A shadow fell over Sonia's face. "Are there any other hotels nearby?"

"Everywhere is full, because of the Festival of the Blood Orange," the concierge replied.

The bloody Festival of the bloody Orange.

"If I may suggest something…" the concierge said. "You'll find that the VIP room has plenty of space for two." She darted a conspiratorial glance at Sonia.

Were the two women in cahoots? How could that be, since he had given Sonia the cold shoulder from their very first meeting? And he hadn't been any nicer to her, especially since the whole trip business had unfolded. When Mrs. Ashcroft had asked him to take Kate's place, Sonia's face had turned into a flashing emergency sign. There was no doubt that she didn't want him on the trip, so how could she possibly want him in her bedroom?

"This is not a conversation we should be having here." Sonia's voice was brittle and her knuckles had turned white around the knife and fork.

They walked out into the corridor, out of the kids' hearing range, the concierge's high-heels clacking apologetically behind them.

"I know it's not ideal," the concierge pressed on, "but it would only be for one night. Some of the guests will check out tomorrow and we'll be able to give you separate rooms then. Of course, we won't charge you for the faulty room. And the VIP suite will be on us, as well, to say sorry for the *inconvenience*."

Was there a shade of sarcasm in that last word?

The gentle curve of Sonia's jaw twitched and her eyes darted to the table where the kids were eating, then to Jake and Katie's table and to the hotel's entrance, as if looking for an answer...for help. "Brad, as you've paid for the suite, the choice has to be yours — if there *is* any choice."

Quite... If there was any choice. Whichever way he twisted this Rubik's cube of a problem — splitting and re-pairing the rooms' occupants in every way — he couldn't find a combination that kept the newlyweds together, the boys and the girls apart and him and Sonia in separate rooms. If the hotel wouldn't allow him to sleep in a cold room, they certainly wouldn't allow him to sleep in the housekeeper's storeroom or on a mat in a corridor. But even though there was no official solution, he could still try an 'unofficial' route, provided he kept it quiet. "That's fine. We'll share for one night."

Satisfied, the concierge left them. Instead of returning to the table with Sonia, Brad rushed upstairs. If he got to room three-o-five before they changed the lock's code, he'd sleep there. Unfortunately, the first thing he saw when he got out of the lift was his suitcase huddled outside the door. Sure enough, when he tapped the card against the lock, a red light flashed. The concierge had gotten there before him. He leaned against the wall and let out a sigh. It wouldn't be fair to ask any of the boys to host him on the floor of their room. Stiff upper lip and all that, he just had to resign himself to sharing with Sonia. With some luck, the VIP suite would have more than one space, maybe an anteroom or at least a partition behind which he could camp out, keeping Sonia out of his sight.

* * * *

This was exactly the 'double date' situation Sonia had dreaded—Jake and Katie, Brad and her, all in the lift together, heading for their adjacent VIP suites. Jake and Katie with their hands in each other's back pockets like a two-for-one bundle, Brad and her with their hands white-knuckle tight around their suitcases' handles—one couple as eager to get into their suite as the other was reluctant to step into theirs.

Sonia would have happily moved in with some of the girls if she hadn't thought that it was unfair to them. No matter how hard she tried, she couldn't think of a rooming combination that didn't negatively affect other people. All she could hope for was that they'd find more than one room in the VIP suite—a sofa in an entrance hall, perhaps? In all likelihood, she'd still have to share a bathroom with Brad. The tanned, toned torso she had glimpsed on the airplane flashed across her mind before she wrestled it back into her own mental Pandora's box.

Brad was gazing at the scrolling floor display like a stock trader enraptured by share prices. Sonia would have followed it too, but even the possibility of their lines of sight crossing made her uncomfortable. The lift was too small.

You're breathing the air that's just been in his lungs. She sneaked a hand into her handbag and wrapped it around her inhaler.

Not a moment too soon, the doors opened and Sonia was the first out into a corridor that was paved with cheerful yellow, white and blue ceramic tiles. Bouquets of honeysuckle and lavender in brightly colored vases sat on bow-legged consoles, spreading their delicious scents into the air. This was clearly a special floor. The doors of the two suites were adjacent. *Great.* They'd have to hear the creaking of Jake and Katie's bed.

"Breakfast is at seven-thirty, right?" Jake asked, visibly impatient to get through the door and shut it firmly behind.

"Do you need us to wake the kids in the morning?" Katie offered.

It was kind of her, but Sonia was determined to give the newlyweds the honeymoon she had promised and to reserve their help for absolute emergencies. "No need, thank you. Brad and I will do it. Unless, for some reason, we don't wake up, in which case, please, come wake us." She hadn't even finished saying it, when she realized how dodgy that sounded, and her face flared. "Of course, there's no reason why we shouldn't wake up—I mean, only if both our alarms failed…" She was digging herself in deeper.

"Of course, it can happen." Katie flashed her a smile and a wink.

"No chance. I've packed a backup alarm," Brad said curtly.

Sonia felt like the protagonist of the story of *The Woman Who Was Swallowed Up by the Floor and Who Met Lots of Other Women Down There Too*. "Excellent!" she shrilled, "Goodnight, then."

"Goodnight!" Jake and Katie echoed cheerfully, opening the door to their suite.

Sonia tapped her quivering key card against the lock of her and Brad's suite. The green light flashed, she pushed the door and her jaw dropped.

Chapter Four

An emperor-sized four-poster bed, wrapped in baby-blue tulle curtains, sat on a dais like a throne. Heart-shaped chocolates in crinkly pink foil drew a giant heart on the immaculate white linen. A picture on the wall opposite read "...*e vissero felici e contenti*"... 'and they lived happily ever after'.

This was the honeymoon suite. Sonia's heart sank to the pit of her stomach. *There must be a mistake. This must be Jake and Katie's room.* She whipped around and dashed through the crack of Jake and Katie's slowly closing door shouting, "There's been a mistake!" but froze halfway in. The couple was already coiled together in a tangle of limbs on a bed identical to the one next door.

"Ahem...on reflection...er, our rooms are the same. No worries, no mistake. Other than mine, of course, barging in on you..." *Shut up!* Sonia backed out and pulled their door shut against the spring.

Righto. So Jake and Katie's suite was exactly the same, which was great news for them but not quite so great for her and Brad.

Sleeping with him in a twin room would have been horrible enough, but sharing a flipping honeymoon suite? It added insult and cringe to bloody injury. She scanned the space for other rooms, corridors, halls, walk-in cupboards—anything where she could carve herself a private space. *Nothing.* The suite was open plan. As her gaze met the frosted glass screen which separated the marble bathtub and toilet, she almost cried. Damn, even the bathroom was open plan! If the architect had been within arm's reach, she would have strangled him. It must have been a 'him'.

Brad's forehead was scrunched into a frown and he scanned the room like a trapped animal looking for a gap in the fence. "I see," he rasped, when his gaze landed on the open-plan bathroom. He marched up to the turquoise French shutters and pushed them open. An icy breeze wafted in. The moon shimmered on the ceramic tiles that covered the large balcony outside.

"Perfect," he muttered to himself.

What could possibly be 'perfect' in all this? Sonia watched him march to a small blue-and-white floral sofa that sat prettily in a corner and pick it up as if it was no heavier than a suitcase.

"What are you doing?"

He regarded her as if the answer was plainly obvious. "You're having the bed. I'm taking the sofa."

"Where to?"

"Outside."

"Are you kidding?"

"I've slept outdoors before."

"I don't question that, but we're not in Africa. It's still April, the nights are nippy and you haven't got a sleeping bag. Plus, the sofa is too short for you. You take the bed and *I'll* sleep on the sofa — but indoors, if you don't mind."

"I do. I'm a man, not a beast."

Sonia wondered which part of her suggestion — her taking the sofa or her sleeping indoors — he minded. Assuming it was the first, she added, "It's very gallant of you, but we're colleagues. Equality in the workplace goes both ways."

"I hereby declare that I willingly and freely choose the sofa and I acquit you of any accusations of sexual discrimination."

Sonia's hair stood on end. It irked her when he'd gone all formal on her. "If you really want the sofa, that's fine, but at least sleep inside. I'm a woman, not a beast."

"That, I have surely noticed." A mischievous look flashed across his face for a millisecond. Could that have been a double entendre? No, it wouldn't be like Brad.

"I'll be just fine on the terrace," he said curtly, as if he didn't want to discuss the matter further.

"All right. I can't stop you. But I don't like it a bit. If you catch something and fall sick, it'll be a problem for us."

"Sicknesses are caused by germs, not cold air."

"Not in Italy, they're not. Drafts of cold air to the neck can kill, at least according to my mother."

The corners of his mouth flickered into a smile but he continued carrying his stuff outside. Why was he so doggedly insistent on sleeping out in the dew and the cold? Was it chivalry or fear that she'd make advances on him if he stayed indoors? She had met controlling men, predatory men, opportunistic men and manipulative men, but she'd never men who were scared of her. She watched in disbelief as he carried his suitcase out onto the terrace too. *Don't tell me that he's going to get changed on the balcony.* He was, literally, moving out without having ever moved in. "Would you like to get changed in the bathroom before you settle outside?"

He hesitated, glancing at the frosted glass pane.

"I'll go on the balcony and watch the stars for a little while," she offered, to give him some privacy.

"Thank you."

On her way out, she was careful not to cross him at the narrow French doors and made sure to give him a wide berth as they exchanged places. She sensed that, under the circumstances, any kind of proximity would be fraught with meaning and tension.

The balcony was beautiful. Two ceramic flowerpots in the shape of a male and a female head sat on the parapet holding cascading geraniums like cornucopias. The sky above glittered with stars and the scent of the wisteria climber mingled with the perfume of the orange blossom and filled the air with sweetness. Childhood memories of summer nights with uncles, aunts and cousins, playing guitar and tambourines under a starry summer sky, flooded back. This was the Sicily she wanted to reconnect to—not the Sicily of prejudice, patriarchism and a misplaced sense of honor, the Sicily that made an intact hymen a necessary requisite for marriage, the Sicily where women had no choices and lived to serve the men and the Sicily where loving too soon, too late or the wrong person was a worse crime than killing a daughter, a wife or a sister.

Making peace with her heritage was going to take some intricate and taxing heart-work. The last thing she needed was Brad's proximity fogging her mind.

The last time she had found herself in a bedroom alone with a man, it had sparked a catastrophic avalanche of events. Twelve years on, she still had nightmares about the pain that had followed. The what-ifs still haunted her. What if she had been brave enough to run away from home? She would have missed her GCSEs and maybe never gone to university, but she could have kept her baby. Her baby girl would have been as old as her students now. Instead, she was up there with the tremulous stars. All Sonia could do now was to give her students all the love that she would have wanted to give her child. The stars quivered through the film of her teary eyes. *Twinkle, twinkle, little star, how I wonder what you are.* The shutters opened behind her and a shard of light sliced through her.

"You can have the room back. Thank you." Brad's voice reached over her shoulders.

She wiped her eyes with the back of her hand and turned around. Brad was wearing a warm fleece and a baseball hat. Would he be warm enough? Even in the few minutes she'd been out there, a cold breeze had seeped through her clothes and made her shiver. The night was only going to get colder. *Please, Brad, come back inside.* But if she insisted, he'd be convinced that she had a hidden agenda. "Well, goodnight then. If you do change your mind, feel free to come inside. Don't worry. I won't wake up. I'm a heavy sleeper."

He wouldn't need to find out that was a lie.

* * * *

Brad had slipped on an extra pair of socks, a warm fleece and the only hat he had — a baseball cap. But what he really needed was a sleeping bag…or a duvet. Unfortunately, the emperor bed came with an emperor duvet, not two singles. He folded his six-foot-long body into the two-seater sofa and pulled the spare blanket he'd found in the bottom of one of the cupboards over himself. It wasn't going to be a comfortable night, but at least Sonia wasn't within sight and the cold air would cool his senses.

The twinkling stars shed their sidereal light onto the muddle of his heart. Stepping into the room and realizing that it was one of the hotel's honeymoon suites had seemed to shift the floor under his feet. Had he been with anyone — male or female — other than Sonia, he would have cracked a joke. But with her it was different. Panic and desire had chased each other like a cat running after its own tail, his head running away, his body yearning to grab the opportunity.

Not that he thought he had any chance with Sonia. He'd heard her horrified gasp when she took in the four-poster bed — definitely wide enough for two — and the chocolate heart. He had noticed her desperate glance at Jake and Katie's closing door. Now he was completely convinced that Sonia had not orchestrated the room-sharing situation. That thought pushed a little wedge of sadness into his heart, followed by guilt. What the hell was wrong with him? Hadn't he had enough grief in his life? Couldn't he see that his heart couldn't take loving again? Plus, he certainly didn't deserve Sonia. A man who has killed his girlfriend, even accidentally, didn't deserve a second chance. He *must* keep himself at a safe distance from Sonia. He *must* get his own room ASAP.

A good night's sleep was the best ingredient for keeping a level head. He closed his eyes and thought of DNA replication. It was usually conducive to sleep. But, this time, from DNA replication he moved on to gamete formation and, from that...to the extremely attractive woman sleeping in the bed built for two on the other side of the French shutters, in his straight line of sight. Thank goodness he couldn't see through the tilted wooden slats.

Unfortunately, he could imagine. Pictures of her lovely shoulders in the spaghetti-strap dress, of the bikini that had jumped out of her suitcase, of her delicate hands grasping the airplane's armrest, whirled in his mind. The skin of her wrists had felt so smooth and firm that it had set his senses on fire. He shook his head and turned around to face the sky.

Forgive me, Frances. Frances didn't deserve to be replaced like that. And *he* didn't deserve a replacement. If he hadn't been able to take good care of Frances, he didn't deserve to be entrusted with another woman. He closed his eyes and let hot guilt brim over his eyes.

The creaking of the French doors sent his pulse spiking. He shut his eyes firmly and pretended to sleep. He recognized Sonia's gait in the swishing of fabric, smelled her unique scent and felt her presence. He was aching to open his eyes and see the expression on her face, her lovely body in her nightwear. *Dangerous thought.* Pretending to sleep was much safer. A gentle weight descended on his body and warmth seeped into him. He felt her hands tuck under his side and his muscles twitched to pull her into him. He'd kiss her under the stars until there was not a drop of pain left in his heart. *Don't. Don't stir. Don't move.*

When she pulled away, he waited for the creaking of the French doors as she went back inside, but there was no sound other than the croaking of the tree frogs. She must have stopped to admire the sky. A little later, he finally heard the shutters close. Just in case, he waited a long time before opening his eyes and discovering that she had wrapped him in her duvet. Her warmth was still trapped in the fibers. Now that he was warm enough to sleep, he couldn't. A riot was raging in his heart.

* * * *

She waited a long time to make sure that he was deeply asleep before slipping out onto the balcony to give him her duvet. Of course, in the morning he'd find out what she'd done, but she could deal with that. What she *couldn't* do was to face him in her dressing gown in the middle of the night. It would be way too intimate. Plus, he might refuse her offer. By giving him the emperor duvet, she was left with nothing, because the room's occupants were meant to share both bed and bedding. The thought sent a tingle up her spine…a naughty tingle.

Never mind about her… At least *she* was indoors. She'd wrap up in the bathrobe and the bath towels — both highly unlikely to be used for bathing so long as Brad and she were sharing. She had planned to double the duvet over Brad, tuck him in and scuttle back into her bed, where she'd sleep the peaceful sleep of the virtuous.

But her plan had had a glitch. Like Orpheus had turned around to look at Eurydice, Sonia too let her eyes linger on Brad's beautiful face — and she had been bewitched. Instead of slipping back indoors, she let her gaze caress the lashes arrayed on his cheeks, glistening in the light of the stars. She lingered over the perfect angle of his jaw, much gentler now that he wasn't scowling at her. She admired the lovely curve of his lips, full in all the right places. She drank him in greedily, knowing that she couldn't do it when he was awake.

You can't want this man. She didn't do men anymore, and this one was a colleague too. *A double no.* Experience had shown her that men loved her and left her, like the father of her baby, who had fled at the news of her pregnancy. *He was only sixteen.* All right, some men stuck around and built their lives with their women, but that wasn't better either. The women would find themselves chained to the kitchen stove, with only enough slack to reach the sink, like her mum. Her dad loved her with all his heart and he'd readily jump into fire and water for her. Still, his adoration hadn't stopped him from pushing her into a life of subservience. And there was not a drop of adoration in the man sleeping before her.

She shivered as the cold night air seeped into her dressing gown, and she'd slunk back inside. Instead of descending into the peaceful sleep of the virtuous as she'd planned, she lay awake staring at the French doors for a very long time.

The first glow of dawn woke her—or maybe it was the cold. Bath towels, it seemed, weren't as warm as duvets or even blankets. If she was cold indoors, was Brad frozen out there? She tiptoed to the French window, gingerly tilted the slats of the blinds and peered through. The low rays of sun skimmed the top of a citrus orchard. It was a dark green blanket peppered with the little white *zagara* flowers. Brad was standing at the parapet, gazing into the sunrise. She pulled away from the shutters as if they had burned her fingers. Heaven forbid he caught her snooping.

He must be waiting for me to wake up. She quickly used the bathroom and slipped into her clothes for the day. She would have very much appreciated a shower, but not at the price of keeping him out in the cold for any longer than necessary. Her shower could wait till the evening, when they'd get their own rooms. She ran a hand through her hair, checked herself in the mirror, then opened the French doors. "Hi."

He turned around and looked at her as if she'd just pulled him back from a very distant place. The hand he ran through his disheveled hair made no difference. It was still cutely messy, with a coppery glimmer drawn out by the sun brushing it at an angle. The slanting sun rays also made his irises look like pools of transparent turquoise water. The balcony's tiles seemed to shift under Sonia's feet.

"Good morning," he said, in an early morning croak. "Thank you for the duvet." He smiled and lovely little creases fanned out to the sides of his eyes.

Sonia's breath snagged in her throat. *Don't you get weak at the knees about him.* Her muscles tensed. "I'm the kind of person who can't pass by a homeless man without giving away her lunch," she scoffed.

Hurt flashed across his eyes and his gaze hardened.

She felt instantly ashamed. What was she thinking, implying that her gesture had been an act of charity? "I hope you were not too cold," she whispered, trying to patch things up.

"I was just fine."

Whether his night had been icy or not, his voice was, and Sonia was overcome with the urge to run away. "I'd better go down and check on the breakfast."

Chapter Five

The breakfast table was a cornucopia of local produce. From the oversized *cedro* lemons with their deliciously thick, soft pith to the fresh ricotta cheese that tasted like milk, from the freshly baked bread buns that smelled heavenly to the sweet yellow loquats, everything was laid out like an offering to the gods. In that kaleidoscope of colors, the place of honor — on a cake stand, no less — was taken by slices of Tarocco blood orange. Resentful of their role in the room shortage, Sonia dodged them and took a handful of early season cherries instead.

With a bowl of yogurt, her cherries and a small pastry, she sat down at a table where Charlotte, Laura and Hazel were sitting. "Did you sleep well, girls?"

"Yes, Miss, thank you," Hazel replied politely. "How about you?"

"Me too, thanks," she lied. When would she learn not to ask questions that she didn't want to be turned to her?

"What's this giant lemon?" Laura asked, pointing to the *cedro* on Sonia's plate.

"A *cedro*. This is how you eat it." Sonia shook the saltshaker over the white and yellow slices on her plate and offered some to the girls.

"Salt?"

"Yes. Try it."

Charlotte bit into it. "That's actually nice!"

"I'm going to get my own," Laura said.

"Me too. Let's go?" Hazel and Laura left the table and joined the queue at the buffet, leaving Charlotte and Sonia alone.

"How are you today, Charlotte?" Sonia noticed that Charlotte was wearing her own clothes today, which was reassuring, but she decided against asking for her own clothes back yet.

"Much better than you, Miss." Charlotte looked into Sonia's bowl, which was empty, apart from a few cherry seeds. "When I was small, my granny would count the fruit stones on my plate singing *tinker, tailor…* Do you know this rhyme?"

"No, I don't. Both my grannies were Italian. Teach me."

"Okay. It goes like this."

"Tinker,
Tailor,
Soldier,
Sailor,
Rich man,
Poor man,
Beggar man,
Thief."

Tinker, Tailor, Soldier...Sailor. Phew! Sailor is not as good as 'rich man', but it's better than 'beggar man' or 'thief'. Just then, Brad came into the dining room, looking gorgeous with his mussed hair and rumpled jeans. Charlotte jumped from her chair and pointed at him. "Of course! Mr. Wilson is a sailor."

"You've lost me, Charlotte."

"Sorry, Miss. I forgot to say that the rhyme tells you who you're going to marry."

Sonia felt her cheeks flame. "I'm not intending to marry anyone. Come on. Finish up your breakfast. We have a busy day ahead."

* * * *

Breakfast had been easy. Sitting with the boys, Brad had feasted on freshly baked Sicilian bread and local cheese. Now they were on the coach, headed for Palermo, and he hoped to snatch a couple of hours' sleep to make up for the short night. He was comfily nestled in his usual seat but sleep didn't come. Questions whizzed around his head instead. He remembered the tender pressure of Sonia's hands tucking the duvet around his body. It had been a loving, caring gesture. But why did she brush it off with a joke about homeless people? More importantly, why had her joke hurt him?

After half an hour, he gave up on sleeping and looked out of the window. As they descended from the Madonie mountains toward the sea, prickly pear cacti peppered the side of the roads with their brightly-colored flower buds, interspersed with patches of fluffy chick-yellow acacia blossoms. The sun glittered on the sea like specks of pure gold. Sicily was as beautiful as they'd told him.

Eventually, the motorway poured into Palermo and their coach joined the chaos of the city's traffic — vehicles overshooting traffic lights, scooters weaving through moving cars only millimeters away from wing mirrors and bonnets, pedestrians appearing from between parked cars. The sight of a girl riding on the back of a motorcycle without a helmet froze Brad's blood. Blowing in the wind, her ginger hair — the same color as Frances' — triggered a flashback. If Frances had worn a helmet that day, she might have survived.

What-ifs pave the way to despair.

He turned the other way, where Sonia was looking out of the window. They'd have their work cut out keeping the children together and safe in this chaotic city. And doing it on the few hours' sleep he had managed to snatch would be harder still. Thank goodness the concierge had promised to give him a room when he got back that evening.

The first stop was the Norman Royal Palace.

From the outside, it looked like a hodgepodge of buildings squashed into each other, a cacophony of stone and mortar thrown together in different centuries. But beyond the strange façade, a beautiful courtyard opened before them. Sonia led them in, while Brad brought up the rear, keeping a bodyguard's watch on the group.

Each floor had a corridor running around the balustrade, walked by men in suits, since the palace was still in use as the seat of the regional government. But the first floor's corridor was extra special. Golden mosaics spilled out into the corridor like music wafting out of a room. It was the entrance to what had been the personal chapel of the Norman kings.

As they walked in, the children gasped in surprise. In stark contrast with the outside's hustle and bustle, the chapel was a sanctuary of silence and beauty — a perfect little jewel. Every surface was clad in golden mosaics. Arab, Byzantine and Norman architecture mingled together in a dance of beauty. Islamic motifs decorated the floors, a spectacular muqarnas ceiling took their breath away and mosaics of Bible scenes ran along the side walls. It was a shining example of Arab and Western culture cohabitating peacefully and complementing each other. Brad wondered if the Arabs and the Normans of the times intermarried. He imagined an Arab woman who looked like Sonia marrying a Norman man who looked like him. Sonia intercepted his gaze and he realized that he'd been staring at her.

Stop it.

"Isn't this place beautiful?" Katie asked him, while Jake was taking pictures.

"Yes. Very."

"This trip is turning out even better than I had imagined. How about for you?" Her eyes were a little too bright, her gaze a little too penetrating.

He shifted on his feet. "Yes, Sicily is very beautiful."

"And Sicilian women… Don't you think they're quite pretty too?" Her gaze hopped to Sonia — who was translating a Latin inscription for the children — then back to him. The light reflected by the mosaics gave her skin a golden glow. Yes, he found his colleague beautiful, but that was only one of the qualities that attracted him. She was intriguing, surprising, generous to a fault and her whole being hummed with incredible energy. How could a woman so petite, almost doll-like, give out so much raw energy? Could he tell Katie? No. But Brad never lied. Not since, as a child, his classmates had asked him if he fancied a certain girl and he had denied it out of embarrassment. She had burst into tears. From that day on, he had always kept quiet if he couldn't tell the truth.

Katie must have read the answer to her question on his face, because she smiled and walked away.

Outside the palace, an Ape three-wheeler was parked on the pavement. It had been specially modified so that the back carried a cauldron of simmering cooking oil. The smell of freshly fried fritters was enough to make the pavement drool. *"Panelle e crocché?"* the man sang in a tenor voice.

"Can we try them?" the children clamored.

Sonia consented, and they had an unplanned but delicious snack of chickpea flour fritters and potato croquette sandwiches. Then they visited the cathedral, followed by lunch in a nearby *trattoria* and a walk to a family-run puppet theatre in the old town, to watch a show of traditional Sicilian puppets.

Knight puppets in clanging armor fought each other with loud clashing and shouting, while clouds of dust lifted off the wooden stage as the puppeteers stamped their feet for extra sound effects. Painted wooden heads rolled off the stage, some landing into the laps of the electrified children, and bodies were split in half along pre-made red-painted cuts, as Saracen and Carolingian knights jousted for the hand of the King of Cathay's daughter, the beautiful Angelica. The kids gasped, booed and shouted like in a pantomime. Brad noticed Sonia joining in too. But when the cloud of dust that had lifted off the stage spilled onto the audience, he saw her whip her inhaler out of her handbag. Was she having an asthma attack?

Brad was about to stand up and shout to the puppeteers to stop lifting dust, when the death of a character brought the battle to an abrupt end. Sonia took a last couple of puffs and put her inhaler away. He wanted to ask her if she felt okay, but she was sitting at the other end of the row in front and he couldn't reach her. Not long after, the story ended with the Knight Orlando losing his wits over his unrequited love for Angelica.

Let it be a lesson.

Brad was keen to leave that dingy, dusty place, but they still had to visit the puppeteers' workshop. There, they tried holding up and handling the twelve-pound puppets, which wasn't as easy as it looked. Everyone seemed to enjoy it, but Brad was on edge. The workshop was full of sawdust and he didn't want Sonia to suffer an asthma attack. He breathed a sigh of relief when they finally left.

By then, it had started to drizzle. Robin, who shouldn't get his ears wet for medical reasons, had forgotten his waterproof jacket in the hotel. Brad lent him his hooded jacket and they all continued their exploration of the city's historical quarters, between statues-adorned fountains, baroque churches and Arabic buildings. The architecture was beautiful, but Brad paid only limited attention, as he kept a relentless watch over the group. The whizzing scooters, the faded pedestrian crossings and the narrow pavements with stone edging made slippery by the rain all kept him on edge. After a few hours, he was soaked, cold and tired. Thank goodness he'd be getting his own room that evening. He longed for a hot shower and a warm bed.

As he watched the children make a beeline for Sonia on the narrow pavement, something in his field of view jarred. Observing the traffic around them, he had worked out that, if Sicilians wore any helmets at all, they used half-face helmets on scooters and full-face ones only on big, powerful bikes. There in front of him were two men, illegally riding a scooter made for one, donning full-face helmets. Another oddity was that they were skimming the pavement, although there was plenty of space on the empty road. As they rode toward them, milliseconds before the passenger stretched out his arm, Brad knew.

"Don't you dare!" he roared, as the man grabbed Sonia's bag.

Startled by Brad's shout, the rider wobbled. Sonia clutched her bag, but the thief had already clamped his hand around the strap and had the advantage of the momentum. Sonia was dragged to the ground before she let go of her bag.

Raw, primeval fury deflagrated in Brad's chest. "You bastard!" He leaped at the snatcher and punched him so hard on the helmet that the scooter wobbled out of control. The man yelped and let go of the bag while his accomplice accelerated away, Italian curses wafting out of their helmets.

One of the kids snatched the bag from the ground. Brad rushed to Sonia.

"Are you hurt?" he panted. His heart had run off at a gallop and every drop of tiredness, hunger and cold had evaporated from his body.

"I'm fine, totally fine," she said, her eyes open wide and palms thrust out in a *don't-touch-me* sign.

She looked scared. He had overreacted. His aching fist also told him that much. Recovering Sonia's bag back would have been enough. Punching and swearing had been over the top. But when he had seen her being pulled to the ground, he'd lost the light of reason. *Knight Orlando lost his mind because of a woman.* It was the same rage that welled inside him each time he remembered the accident, each time he relived his powerlessness before the motorbike had spun out of control and crushed Frances. He must be getting worse rather than better, if the sight of any woman in distress gave him flashbacks. *But Sonia is not any woman.* Sonia was just a colleague. They weren't even friends. *But my heart stammers every time I'm close to her.*

Sonia got up, dusted down her jeans and looked straight into his eyes. Her irises flowed deep and velvety like molten dark chocolate.

I like her too much.

She cleared her throat. "Thank you for —"

"No worries," he interrupted. "I'm just the kind of man who can't help running after old ladies' bag-snatchers."

* * * *

Touché. After her homeless joke, she only had herself to blame for him having a dig at her. But it still stung. She didn't mind being compared to a little old lady, but she would have liked to think that he cared about her personally, rather than that he had stepped in just because he was a serial hero.

While the coach trundled up the mountain and everyone who wasn't talking about Brad's valiant rescue was asleep — including him — Sonia replayed the incident in her mind.

She couldn't work him out. One moment he gave her the impression that being on the trip with her was close to torture, and the next moment he lashed out at a bag-snatcher with the fury of a parent who had seen their child being attacked. One could almost think that he was being...protective.

The closest human relationship she could think of to make sense of Brad's behavior was that of Sicilian brothers with their younger sisters. They found their sisters insufferable but wouldn't allow anyone to hurt them.

Still, Brad was as far from a Sicilian man as Sonia was from the Queen. There was no impulsivity, no emotion about him. Everything he did or said was always rational, restrained, ruminated. Chasing after scooter-riding bag-snatchers and punching them was completely out of character for him.

Or is there more to him than meets the eye? Sonia wished she could see through his armor. Instead, all she could see was his chest rising and sinking as he slept. And the worst thing was that she longed to stroke it.

When they finally reached the hotel, they lugged themselves out of the coach and regrouped in the lobby. Brad was soaked like a newborn chick. Not for nothing but the Sicilians called that soft drizzle *assuppaviddranu*, 'farmer-soaker' in dialect. His T-shirt stuck to his chest, leaving little to the imagination, and his wet fringe hung in strands over his forehead, like arrows pointing to his incredible eyes.

"If you want to get changed, go on, and I'll look after the kids. Join us in the restaurant when you're ready," she offered.

"Thanks," he said. "Even us hobos like a shower every now and then."

He smiled mischievously and she rolled her eyes. How many times would he make her regret that joke?

"I'll get the keys to my room," he said.

His room? Of course. Sonia remembered the receptionist reassuring them that they'd only have to share for one night. A ridiculous pin of sadness pricked her. She shouldn't feel anything other than relief and happiness at getting her duvet and bathroom back to herself. All the same… She watched him walk up to the reception desk as if he was emigrating to a distant land.

Don't be stupid.

"Right, everybody. Let's go to the restaurant for dinner," she told the group, and everybody followed her eagerly. But the waitress informed them that their tables weren't quite ready.

"Let's go back to our rooms and freshen up or rest for a quarter of an hour. I'll meet you all back here at eight o'clock," she told everyone.

"Oh, no, Miss. We're hungry," Aidan complained.

"I could eat a house I'm so hungry," Charlotte protested.

"We haven't had anything since lunch," Hazel moaned.

"I'm starving," Robin echoed.

"Robin, you're lucky that Mr. Wilson gave you his raincoat or you would be soaked as well as hungry."

Robin took a step back, looking suitably sorry, although Sonia wasn't sure whether he was sorry for Brad or for himself. Then she opened her bag and produced a packet of grissini sticks, which she had bought for emergencies like this. Luckily there were enough to give one to each child. "Now, off you go to your rooms to wash off the sand."

Walking back past reception, she darted a furtive glance at the desk but didn't see Brad. He must have gotten his key.

She carried on to the lift, wondering if she had enough time to squeeze in a quick shower and slip into a clean dress. Maybe she could even tie her hair up and put on some makeup. It was evening, after all.

When she opened the door of her suite, she was so absorbed in her plans that she didn't think anything of the fact that a key card had already been slotted into the light switch.

Chapter Six

The bed had been made and Sonia flopped backward onto the downy duvet. *Aaah.* Finally, relief for her back. As well as grazing her elbow and bruising her wrist, she had hit her back when the robber had pulled her to the ground. But she had been careful not to let Brad know, in case he ran after the scooter and walloped the guys a little more — bless him, he *was* sweet — or asked to check her back.

His wrist massage on the airplane had caused enough havoc in her belly, as had the wet T-shirt clinging to his pecs after the rain. The guy was too gorgeous for his own good — for *her* own good.

She closed her eyes and stretched her arms above her head, opening her chest and flattening her shoulder blades. She could feel her spine relax and her vertebrae pull away from each other. A groan of pleasure floated from her throat.

She took a deep breath in and a smell of sandalwood floated into her nostrils. What was that? Her curious eyes fluttered open and, looking down between the swell of her breasts, she saw Brad.

A lot of him.

Rivulets of water ran down his neck and bare torso while, with one hand, he clutched the ends of a towel that barely reached around his loins. He stood still before her, statuesque like a perfect Michelangelo masterpiece.

Sonia blinked, her breath caught in her throat, and if she hadn't been lying down, her jaw might have fallen off her face. She whipped herself up to a sitting position. Six feet of hard muscle, masculine beauty and water droplets stood a few inches from her — within arm's reach. Words she had heard many times as a child, *si guarda ma non si tocca* — you can look but you can't touch — rang loud in her ears.

"Weren't you going to dinner?" His tone was accusing.

"S-sorry. The tables weren't ready... I thought they'd given you another room," she stammered, her spine tingling and her eyes disobeying the command to look away. *Leave. Give the guy some privacy.* Her legs wouldn't obey, either. All she could do was dig her nails into her palms and think of England.

"The hotel is full again. We have to share for another night," he said without expression.

He bent down to pick up his clothes from the floor and the edges of the towel parted, exposing a solid, muscly thigh. Sonia couldn't think of England hard enough.

He walked to his suitcase. "But they've given us a folding bed," he continued in a level tone, as if he were fully clothed. Was this like the tale of the *Emperor's New*

Clothes? There was no way that she could pretend that he was fully dressed and stay sane.

She averted her gaze and rested it on the trouser press at the opposite end of the room. *This appliance must be grounded*, the red-and-white sticker warned. The same could have been said about her.

"And a complimentary bottle of limoncello," he finished.

She saw an artisanal-looking bottle of yellow liqueur sitting on the console, with two small glasses tied together with a blue ribbon.

Brad had now gathered his clothes and was clutching them in front of him like a shield, clearly waiting for her to leave.

She swallowed. "Well…I guess I'll be back later… When it's time to drink the limoncello." *What the hell am I saying?* "I mean, I'll see you in the restaurant." *With clothes on. Please.* She peeled her eyes off him and got up, but her legs wouldn't walk her to the door.

He nodded for her to go. "See you downstairs."

She eventually reached the door and closed it firmly behind her. Sharing a room with Brad that night was going to be very tricky.

* * * *

Should he have warned her that they hadn't given him a room? But she was supposed to wait for him in the restaurant! He couldn't be expected to go looking for her, just to say, "Please don't walk on me while I'm having a shower and throw yourself on the bed, moaning and writhing around." Maybe he should have given her the customary cough warning before…before stepping out from behind a barely frosted-glass screen?

Before she had even entered the room? Should he have written a note on the door — *Inside, having a shower* — for anyone walking past to see it too?

In truth, he hadn't noticed her until he had walked out of the shower and found her stretched across the bed, with her ebony curls splayed over the duvet and the swell of her chest rising and sinking as she groaned. No cough could have come out, because his breath had snagged in his throat.

He stepped into a clean pair of jeans and pulled on a long-sleeved top. The air had turned chilly and big, fat raindrops were battering the citrus blossom. It would be impossible for him to sleep outside tonight. He had no choice but to sleep in the room with her. If only the bed's curtains were made of a more substantial fabric than tulle. The heavy velvet of theatre curtains would do, but something sturdy — maybe chainmail — would be even better.

He left the suite and called the lift. The doors opened and Jake and Katie stepped out.

"Hi, Brad. You don't need to go down yet. Dinner has been put off to eight o' clock," Jake informed him.

Katie looked at him through narrowed eyes. "Are you and Sonia sharing the suite tonight too?"

"The hotel is still full," he answered gruffly, inspecting the buttons inside the lift.

Katie gave him a meaningful look. "If neither of you have a room downstairs with the kids, there's no reason why you two should be on duty again tonight." She glanced at Jake, who nodded. "It's our turn now. You can have a night off. We'll tell the kids to come to us if they need anything, and nobody will disturb you unless the building is on fire."

"There's no need. I don't mind night duty." He could see what game Katie was trying to play. He had noticed before that some women, once they'd reached their own romantic happiness, were eager to play matchmaker for others.

"But it's not fair," she piped. "I insist."

"You can't go against this one when she sets her mind on something," Jake warned him.

"Look at it this way, Brad," she went on, eyes sparkling. "If the kids come looking for you at night, they'll find you and Sonia in the same room. We know that it's not been your doing, but people don't ask questions before they start gossiping. If the kids come to us instead, they'll never find out." She smiled with satisfaction while Brad frowned. Objectively, her reasoning made sense.

The lift doors were beginning to close. "I don't know what to say, other than thank you."

"It's our pleasure. See you downstairs."

The rain had stopped and Brad decided to take a stroll in the garden. The smell of wet earth mingled with the heady scents of the citrus and the wisteria blossoms. The air was much warmer than it had been the night before—the hot *scirocco* wind was on its way, the concierge had told him—and the sky sparkled with constellations at the far end from a white sliver of moon. He was always amazed at nature's power to make him feel better.

At eight o'clock he walked into the restaurant. Sonia, Jake, Katie and the kids were already sitting at their tables. Some of the children saw him from a distance and cheered, "Mr. Wilson the avenger?"

Oh, please. He hated violence and was ashamed of his reaction. He wanted to forget what had happened, and he wished everyone else could do so too.

"Mr. Wilson, weren't you scared that the thieves had a knife or a gun?" Hazel asked him, as he sat down at the table with them.

"I didn't think about it," he said candidly. "What I did was stupid,"

He hadn't had time for questions or fear. Seeing Sonia in danger had flipped a primeval switch inside him and, from then on, he had acted under compulsion. It had never happened before, and seeing it happen had shaken him.

"Was there a lot of money in Miss Alletti's bag?" Ryan asked.

"I don't know."

"Was it about her phone, then?"

"Not at all." For all he cared, that handbag could have been full of snotty tissues. It had been all, entirely, about Sonia. Seeing her knocked to the ground had made him see red. Of course, he couldn't tell the kids. "Her passport might have been in the bag." The passport hadn't been his main concern, but it wasn't a lie.

"Then she'd be stuck in Sicily and you would have to take us home on your own," Ryan concluded.

"With Mr. and Mrs. Jenkins," another boy corrected.

"They're no use to Mr. Wilson. They're always snogging," Ryan said.

"Ryan!" Brad reproached him.

"Isn't it the truth?"

Trust kids to spell things in the crudest way.

The sightseeing must have tired the boys out because they filed into bed without any fuss, straight after dinner, and by nine-thirty, Brad was free. The girls' corridor was silent too. Sonia must have gone to their suite and Brad had no wish to spend any more time there with her than necessary, so he opted for another stroll in the garden. Jake and Katie were on duty, so it would be perfectly all right to make himself scarce until it was time to collapse on the sofa and fall asleep. But first he needed to go up and get his phone, just in case.

He found Sonia hunched over her laptop at a cutesy wrought-iron table that was only big enough for a lamp and a couple of champagne glasses. Her rapt concentration was at odds with the whimsy of her surroundings and the holiday-like carelessness of the curls tumbling out of her pencil-twisted bun.

"Hi. Are all the boys in bed?" she asked, without taking her eyes off the laptop's screen.

"Yup." His fingers ached to stroke the rogue lock of ebony hair that was resting on her shoulders.

"Good, because we have a punishing schedule tomorrow. The visit to the catacombs won't be everyone's cup of tea. I didn't want to go, but the history department has given the kids an assignment about embalming, so we can't skip it. We need to plan for people fainting or just finding the place a bit too much."

"I'll deal with the faintings if you look after the rest of the group."

"Thanks. That can work, provided I'm not one of the casualties." Her half-smile suggested that she was only half-joking.

"You're made of much stronger stuff than that," he let slip.

She hooked one foot behind the other knee. "That's nice to hear. I don't much like the idea of being made of 'sugar and spice and all things nice'."

"No, you're not made of that." *Getting too personal. Treading dangerous ground.* His gaze swept the room in search of a distraction and landed on the limoncello bottle. *That's what she's made of—honey and limoncello, with licorice curls for hair.*

She must have followed his gaze, because she said, "I almost forgot the limoncello. Are we going to sit out on the balcony and try some? Jake and Katie are on duty tonight—"

I was going for a stroll. I only came up to get my phone. Say no. "Why not," he answered instead.

"Not that I'm planning to get plastered, but I need to relax a little."

Brad highly doubted that relaxation would be what he'd get by sitting under the stars with Sonia.

Nonetheless, he carried the bottle and a couple of chocolates outside and she joined him with the glasses. A wrought-iron bench with colorful terracotta tiles for a seat was huddled against the wall and cocooned by the wisteria. It was so small that, when they sat down, he had to cross his legs to avoid contact.

The scirocco wind had teased such heady scents out of the flowers that one could have mapped the garden in the darkness, just from the smell. He poured the limoncello into the glasses and offered her one.

"It's warmer tonight," she said. "It's the scirocco. It might bring us a little sand from the Sahara too. It has always fascinated me, how you can suddenly find a film of golden sand from so far away all over your balcony, your car, your garden…"

"Did you grow up in Sicily?" *Don't ask personal questions.*

"No, but I've come on holiday with my family many times. My parents still come every summer, but I don't anymore." Her jaw twitched.

Why didn't she? Was there someone in her life — another half perhaps, who wanted to travel elsewhere? He couldn't imagine anyone disliking Sicily. "Sicily is beautiful."

"I'm glad you like it" — she took a sip from her glass — "because I had a feeling that you weren't all that keen on this trip."

Ha. It was precisely to avoid sipping limoncello on a balcony with her under a starry sky that he had recoiled from the trip. How could he tell her that she was the reason for his reluctance? That her presence had unsettled him from the moment she'd stepped into the school as a new member of staff?

He was silent. "School trips are not my cup of tea. I need my daily dose of solitude."

She snorted. "Then sharing a room is definitely not your cup of tea."

"No." *Especially sharing with you.* He took a sip from his glass and the zingy sting of the lemon and the alcohol trickled down his throat.

They gazed at the sky for a little while, then she broke the silence. "The Romans used to say *in vino veritas*, in wine lies the truth. Do you reckon that applies to limoncello?"

"I guess we're going to find out."

He took another sip, and she copied him.

"Here it comes," she announced. "I'm sorry about the homeless joke. The truth is that I couldn't sleep, knowing that you were freezing outside."

"No umbrage taken." He hitched a leg over the other knee. "Anyway, giving your lunch to a homeless man because you can't bear knowing that he's hungry... Isn't it the same?"

"Perhaps." She sounded unconvinced. "Now it's your turn."

"To do what?"

"To tell me a limoncello truth. It's shocking that we're on this trip together and we know nothing about each other. The kids know more about us than we do about one another."

"What do they know about me that you don't?"

She tapped her chin. "They told me that you love sailing. I didn't know that."

"But they don't know that I've been a surgeon."

"Why did you leave?" she blurted out, as if the question had been on the tip of her tongue for some time. "Sorry... Forget it."

He took a sip. "I knew you would ask."

"You don't have to answer."

No, he didn't have to answer. But, strangely enough, he wanted to. "I killed my girlfriend." He winced at 'killed', but it was 'girlfriend' that snagged in his throat.

Two beats of silence, then, "How?" There was surprise in her voice but no disgust, reproach or horror.

"A motorbike accident. She was my passenger."

"That's hardly 'killing'."

"She wasn't wearing a helmet. I was."

"Did you stop her from wearing one?"

"No. In fact I offered her mine, but she refused it. She said that it was too tight, that it gave her a headache and it messed up her hair. She wasn't the kind of woman to fuss over her hair, so I should have guessed that they were all excuses to make me wear it."

"I'm sorry, but I don't see how that makes it your fault."

He ran a hand over his face. "*I* was controlling the bike. *I* should have stopped when the taxi turned right in front of us. *I* didn't see his indicator when he started turning because he hadn't seen us coming." Those horrible moments rushed back to him in vivid detail — the screaming, the strident scraping of metal, the world spinning upside down, the blackout. He took a swig of limoncello and savored the burning in his throat. Physical pain drowned out the other kinds, even in pleasant doses.

"I'm really sorry — " Sonia said.

"Not as much as I am."

"But, from what you've told me, I'm certain that you don't qualify as guilty. Trust me. I'm a specialist in guilt and remorse." She took a swig from her glass.

"I should have insisted that Frances wear the helmet."

"She was an adult. Nobody should force another person to do things against their will." A spark of rebellion tinkled in her voice.

"It would have been for her own good."

"Who are we to decide what's good for others? Doctors used to practice bloodletting and lobotomy in the name of the patients' 'own good'." Her voice crackled with fire.

"But Frances would still be alive if I'd given her my helmet," he repeated doggedly.

"How do you know? Both of you could have been killed — or be in a permanent coma or paralyzed." She leaned forward, her whole body humming with energy. "Is that why you left your job, because you felt guilty?"

"Yes. I couldn't accept a salary for saving other people's lives after I'd failed to save the one that, to me, mattered the most."

"So that's why you volunteer for Doctors Without Borders."

"Yes. I'm trying to pay back my debt, if that's even possible."

"What debt?" she challenged, straight-backed at the edge of her seat.

"My debt for being alive."

She took a deep breath and her black curls quivered in the moonlight. "None of us has earned the right to be alive, Brad. We all have the same debt. But your existence is a gift to others, and that automatically cancels your debt. Can't you see how much the children love you?" She sounded almost exasperated.

"I don't deserve their love."

"Very few people in this world deserve anything. All the rest of us must accept what we're given and be grateful."

Her gaze pinned him with all its energy. Why should she care about what he thought of himself? "You are not like me, Sonia. You deserve to be loved."

"What do you know about me?" She pushed back against the backrest and hooked her heels onto the bench, then wrapped her arms around her legs and rested her chin on her knees. "I've done my share of killing too."

"I can't imagine you hurting a fly."

She made a sound he couldn't interpret, drained her glass and stood up. "It's getting chilly. I'm going in."

Brad felt instinctively that she wasn't comfortable with the conversation and decided not to follow her inside. He slouched back on the bench and swirled his glass of limoncello to watch it sparkle in the moonlight.

Wow. He had told her about Frances. And it hadn't hurt anywhere near as much as he'd thought it would. Apart from the people who were in his life at the time, nobody else knew, and he couldn't remember the last time he had spoken Frances' name aloud or mentioned the accident.

He couldn't blame his openness on the alcohol — not so quickly and on a full stomach. The warm night, the scent of the flowers, the moon and the stars must have gone to his head. He would have to be more careful from now on. At this rate, by the end of the trip, he and Sonia would be best friends. He couldn't allow that — not with a woman made of licorice and hot spice, a woman who stirred his blood into crazy whirlpools.

* * * *

As soon as the conversation had veered from his past to hers, Sonia's skin had prickled as if a million ants were crawling over her. Not even her closest friends knew about her abortion. After twelve years, she still couldn't talk about it, so when he'd started to prod, she'd had to get up and go back indoors. But now she felt bad about leaving him out there on his own after what he had just told her.

Now that she knew about his motorbike accident, his broodiness and prickliness made more sense. Constantly carrying the weight of a girlfriend's death would make anyone less than sunny. But he was mistaken. There was nothing he could have done to have prevented that tragedy. If only he could see it that way too. If only she could convince him.

She took a couple of steps back to the French doors and hesitated. No, the moment had past. It would be cruel of her to bring up the accident and force him to discuss it again. She turned around and rummaged inside her handbag for a packet of paracetamol. Her whole body ached. She blamed the night's humidity and the bench's hard tiles until she remembered the bag-snatching incident. Her elbow had swollen now and her back hurt like she'd been whacked with a tennis racket. She found the box of paracetamol and pulled out the blister pack. Empty. *Damn.* Hopefully Brad had some in the first-aid bag.

She popped her head out of the French doors. He was slouched on the bench, feet resting on the rim of a flowerpot, looking into the distant darkness like a Byronic hero. The air smelled strongly of lemon blossom, *zagara,* and Sonia wondered if the Sicilians' belief that *zagara* was an aphrodisiac wasn't an old wives' tale after all. *Stop it, Sonia.* "Have you got any painkillers?" she asked with forced nonchalance.

He started. "Why?"

"Nothing. Just a bit of backache."

He folded his long limbs out of the bench and stood up. "It's the fall you had earlier, isn't it?"

"Have you got any painkillers, yes or no?"

"I'd better check you." He picked up his glass and the bottle and made to go in.

"There's absolutely no need. I'm quite all right. It was just a tingle and it's already fading."

"No, you're not all right. You've been dragged onto the ground and now you're in pain. Backs are delicate things. I need to check you." He pushed past her and marched to his suitcase, from which he pulled out a little doctor's bag.

This was getting beyond ridiculous — first sharing an open-plan honeymoon suite and now having a full-body examination. Would there ever be an end to the cringe? When she'd suggested that they get to know each other a little more, she hadn't meant physically. The images of his wet torso that were singed into her brain were enough trouble already, as was the memory of the wrist massage and of being pressed against him on the plane, when they'd — *Enough.*

He pulled out a stethoscope and a frisson of fear ran up her sore back. Since the abortion, she had developed a phobia of all things medical.

"I don't need painkillers anymore. I'm all better now."

"You can't be. Only two seconds ago you were asking for some." He carried on rummaging in his bag and pulled out a tube of ointment.

"I don't need anything. The limoncello has anaesthetized me." She stepped backward until her sore spine was resting against the cool wall.

His irises seemed to veer from jade green to dusty blue and he pinned her with a stern gaze. "I know that you don't fancy tomorrow's trip, but we need you to come too. Even if you don't care about your back, let me look after it for the sake of the children. They need you to be well until the end of this trip."

He was right. She was being childish and selfish. She stepped away from the wall, squaring her shoulders and thrusting her chin out. "I suppose it's only fair that you see my back after I've seen yours."

"If thinking this way helps you, then by all means."

She sat sideways on the chair by the little table, facing away from him, and started to lift the back of her top. Halfway up, a jab of pain stabbed her, and she sucked in air.

"Let me help you," he said.

He skimmed her skin with his fingers as the fabric glided over her back. It was the gentlest of touches, and it sent the hair follicles all over her body quivering with delight. Her eyes fluttered close.

"Poor thing... You have a nasty bruise," he said tenderly. "Tell me if it hurts when I touch you."

She nodded. His touch did do things to her, but none of them could be called 'hurting'. In fact, he had instantly flushed every pain and ache from her body with a flood of hormones.

"It seems to be only a muscular injury." His voice was a little rough now and a groan that definitely didn't sound like it was from pain escaped his throat. "I should put some ointment on it."

The low rumble of his voice pooled in the pit of her belly like liquid chocolate. "Please, do," she breathed.

As he ran his fingers across her skin ever so delicately, she could tell, like only a woman can, that his was no longer the touch of a doctor. A delicious heat—from the ointment? from his hands?—spread from her back to her entire body, lighting a fire deep inside her that was nothing to do with the limoncello. New and irresistible aches replaced the old ones, aches that could only be soothed by him, but not in a medical capacity.

She was holding on to prudence and sense—or were they holding on to her?— by the thinnest hair. If they let go of her, she would tumble into his arms with the momentum of an avalanche rolling into a valley. She knew there'd be no going back. Avalanches didn't roll back up their cliffs. And still, slowly, inexorably, she turned around.

Her eyes met his—deep, tortured, tragic. And she knew that he wanted her as much as she wanted him. They leaned closer to each other—then someone knocked on the door.

Chapter Seven

She quickly got dressed again and rubbed her cheeks. She couldn't imagine how the hot turmoil that had sent her body's chemistry haywire would have left no traces on her face. When she nodded, Brad opened the door.

Laura Hardman's eyebrows shot up. "Sorry, Mr. Wilson. I thought this was Mr. and Mrs. Jenkins' room."

"They're next door. Do you need anything, Laura?"

The girl caught sight of Sonia. "Oh. Miss Alletti is here too…"'

Only then did it occur to Sonia that it would have been wiser not to be seen in the same room as Brad.

Too late now.

"The hotel is overbooked and they didn't have enough rooms to give us one each," Brad said without missing a beat.

Sonia admired his coolness. She got up and went to the door. "Hello, Laura. Is everything all right?"

Laura was Charlotte's roommate, and that alone gave Sonia a tingle of concern.

"I'm sorry to disturb you. I thought this was Mr. and Mrs. Jenkins' room. I'm worried because Charlotte hasn't come back yet…"

"Come back from where?" Sonia tried to keep the alarm bells under control that were ringing in her head.

"She went downstairs to the vending machine."

There were good reasons why they weren't allowed out of their rooms after the night curfew, but it wasn't Laura who had broken the rule and it wasn't right to reprimand her, not after she had plucked up the courage to raise the alarm for Charlotte. "When did she leave your room?"

"Just after you said goodnight to us."

That had been more than an hour ago. Charlotte could well have left the hotel's grounds in that time. Sonia's heart broke into a gallop. "Thank you for letting us know, Laura. I'm going to look for her. Go back to your room and, if Charlotte comes back, ring this room and tell Mr. Wilson." Then to Brad, "I'm taking my phone."

"I'll go. You stay here."

His offer didn't surprise Sonia but she couldn't accept it. She had made a promise to Charlotte's mother and she must see it through. "Thanks, but I want to go."

"Promise that you'll call me if you need help."

"I will."

The first place she checked was, of course, the vending machine area. A gaggle of boys, who should have been asleep in their rooms, were huddled around the Pringles and the Coca-Colas. As soon they saw her, they burst into excuses about unquenchable thirsts and torturing hunger. But Sonia had no time to scold them. "Have you seen Charlotte Rogers?"

"No, Miss."

"All right. Now off to bed, you lot," she said in a no-messing-with-me tone, and they immediately scuttled to the lifts.

Where could Charlotte be? In somebody else's room, having a little party to which Laura wasn't invited? Sonia took the lift to the third floor and paced the corridor, listening for noises coming through the doors that might indicate that anyone was still awake.

Something was going on in room three-fifteen. Sonia knocked and the chatting and giggling instantly turned into a breathless silence. Nobody came to the door.

Sonia knocked again. "I know that you're awake. Open the door."

There was frantic whispering, the shuffling of slippers then the reluctant click of the door lock.

"Er… Hello, Miss." Tracey was wearing llama pajamas, enormous fluffy slippers that would have taken enough suitcase space for a couple of fleeces and a butter-won't-melt smile — but she had chocolate in the corners of her mouth.

"Who's in this room?"

"Just Millie and me," she said, as if it were obvious.

"Tell me the truth."

"What, Miss? I'm not lying." Tracey lifted her hands in the air and put on the most convincing face of innocence.

But Sonia knew better. She pushed past her and opened the bathroom door. Seven pairs of pupils stared back at her with a mixture of exhilaration and fear. But none of them were Charlotte's.

"Out of here and back to your rooms," Sonia told them calmly. The girls climbed out of the bathtub and sheepishly filed out of the room.

"I didn't know they were there, Miss," Tracey protested, still looking totally innocent.

"In that case, I'd better help you find out if there are any more people hiding in your room."

"No! I mean, there's no need, Miss."

But Sonia was already opening cupboards, lifting beds' valances, discovering more girls in pajamas and packets of chocolate buttons and crisps.

"Everyone back to your room! I want you in bed and asleep within the next two minutes."

Everyone scuttled out of Tracey and Millie's room. What luck was it that almost all the girls on the trip were in that room except Charlotte?

Sonia stood in the corridor, watching the lights in the gaps under the other doors go off, but room three-twelve stayed lit.

Sonia knocked forcefully. No answer. She knocked again. "It's Miss Alletti. Open the door."

A few seconds later, a bleary-eyed Elodie appeared at the door. "Yes, Miss?" She wasn't one of the girls who had been in Tracey's room and, if she was faking having been asleep, she could have won an Oscar.

"Why weren't you in bed?"

"I was."

"Why are your lights on?"

"We're afraid of the dark, Miss." Elodie pushed the door and Sonia saw Lucy wrapped in her duvet, fast asleep, under the blaring light of bedside lamps, fluorescent ceiling light and bathroom lights. The whole gamut was switched on, bright as a galaxy. It was lucky that hotel bills didn't count electricity consumption.

"Is it just you and Lucy?"

"Yes."

"Sorry to disturb you, girls. Goodnight."

Where can Charlotte be? God, not in the boys' rooms, please!

Room three-o-eight was the first of the boys'. There was the unmistakable sound of music. Dubstep. Sonia knocked and the music stopped.

"I know you're awake. Open the door."

There was whispering then silence. Sonia knocked again. Slowly, the door squeaked open onto the same boys she had met by the vending machine. They were standing in a line in front of one of the beds, but Sonia could see through the gaps the cans of Coca-Cola and the crisp packets open and spilling onto the duvet.

"When I told you to go to bed, I meant each in his own bed." Her voice didn't sound as reproaching as she had intended because she was a little relieved not to have found Charlotte rolling on the bed with one of them.

"Sorry. We misunderstood," Ryan said.

"You haven't found Charlotte yet, Miss?" Aidan asked. He didn't sound like he was baiting her—just interested and maybe a little worried.

"No, but I'm finding lots of other people in places where they shouldn't be. Now don't turn that music back on—"

The boys burst into laughter.

"What's funny?"

"The music was Ryan beatboxing."

"Was it good, Miss? Did you think it came from a speaker?" Ryan asked, excitedly.

"To your beds! Now?"

"Yessss, Misss!"

On his way out, Ryan swiped a handful of crisps off the duvet and stuffed them into his mouth. "My throat's a little dry," he said, spluttering crumbs.

Sonia rushed back downstairs. However much it hurt her pride to admit to the receptionist that she had lost one of her pupils, it was necessary.

"Sorry. I haven't seen any girls, just some boys by the vending machines," the man on night duty told her.

The floor seemed to shake under her legs. More than an hour had passed since Charlotte had last been seen, and that was long enough for a girl who felt responsible for her parents' failed marriage, who watched suicide videos... *I've promised to look after her as if she was my own daughter.* Charlotte should be safely tucked in bed in her room. Instead, Sonia had no idea where she was.

She was about to ask the receptionist to call the police when an idea flashed into her mind. She rushed to the double doors that opened onto the back garden but they were shut. She ran out of the main entrance, crossed the *al fresco* terrace, dodging the empty tables, and vaulted the low stone wall into the back garden.

A pair of small shoulders poked out of the top of the same bench where the two of them had chatted on the evening of their arrival. Sonia whipped her phone out of her bag and typed a text for Brad.

I've found her. All is well.

She hesitated, then added,

Don't worry if I'm back late.

It felt strange, as if Brad was someone waiting at 'home' for her, but she was going to give Charlotte all the time she needed.

Immediately, a text pinged back.

Great job. Thanks.
Brad

It was only then that, reading the message she had sent him, she saw her signature and cringed.

Sonia x

The text predictor must have automatically added the kiss. Hopefully he'd know it had been a slip. *But you almost kissed him tonight.*

"Hello, Miss." Charlotte had turned around and was squinting at her against the lights of the hotel's windows. She must have been alerted by the phone's pinging.

"Hello, Charlotte." Sonia didn't think for a moment about scolding her. Instead, she sat on the bench next to her, just like she had done on the evening they had arrived. That bench now felt like it was theirs.

"Are you still keeping an eye on your clothes, Miss?" Charlotte asked.

With a pang, Sonia recognized her jeans and cardigan. It couldn't have been an accident, not for a teen girl who cared about her appearance. Sonia read it for what it was—the girl's plea for Sonia to keep watching over her.

"I'm not. I know that they're in good hands."

"Mine?" The girl snorted. "There's nothing good about me."

"Rubbish."

"Yes, I am," Charlotte said.

"You know what I meant."

"I *am* rubbish. I bring bad things to everyone around me."

"That's your choice. You can make other people happy if you want to."

"No, I can't, Miss. I videocalled Mum after you said goodnight to us. I saw some bin liners in the background, by the door, and I asked her what they were. She said that they were stuff for the dry cleaner, but I knew that she was making it up. It was too much stuff. They were Dad's things, I'm sure. He's taking his chance to move out while I'm here so that he doesn't have to"—her voice trembled—"say goodbye." Her shoulders shook and she burst into sobs.

Sonia hugged her. "I'm sorry, sweetie. You might be right about your dad or you might be wrong, but whatever he's doing, it's not your fault." Sonia's heart cried out for Charlotte and shook her ribs. What kind of a man would hurt his daughter this much, wouldn't love her enough to stay? A man who couldn't stay with his partner because of a child wasn't worthy of either of them.

She squeezed Charlotte tighter as if, doing that, she could drain all the girl's tears, flush out all her pain, scoop her up and press her together so that she wouldn't leak away.

"It's my fault. I should have never been born at all."

Sonia's mind flitted to her unborn girl and she shuddered. Would her daughter have spoken words like that? She chased the thought back into her Pandora's box and steadied her voice. "Don't say that. You can bring a lot of happiness to other people if you want to, and you already do—to your mum, for one. Then, one day, someone will fall in love with you and you'll be the only human being in the whole wide world who can make them truly happy."

"That will never happen." Charlotte wiped her eyes on Sonia's shoulder.

"It will. But you won't notice that it's happening if you keep staring at yourself and only seeing how much you hurt."

Charlotte snuffled quietly and wrapped her arms around her legs.

Sonia leaned back and glanced at the balcony behind them. Up there was a man who also needed to stop staring into his hurting heart. Even though she had sworn never to get close to a man again, she had almost kissed him. And he was sleeping in her room.

Only, he wasn't.

When Sonia had tucked Charlotte into bed and returned to the suite, Brad wasn't there. In the warm light of the bedside lamp that he had left on, she could see no sign of him or his folding bed. She tiptoed to the French doors and, tilting the slabs a little, she saw him asleep on the folding bed out on the balcony, just like the night before.

Disappointment pricked her chest before she could rub it away. *What was I thinking? Did I expect to return and pick up where we'd left off?* Heaven had sent Laura to save her from a huge mistake in the nick of time, and she was keen to go for it all over again? She bit her lips in self-punishment.

Look at him, sleeping like a baby. I've misread him. If he had been interested in her, he would have waited. She must have completely misunderstood the situation. But the look in his eyes…? *I'm deluding myself.*

Her backache had returned with a vengeance, sinking its sharp teeth into her flesh. The ointment must have worn off. She really could do with some painkillers. She struggled into her pajamas, cursorily brushed her teeth and dragged herself to the bed.

On her bedside table, beside a glass of water, lay a packet of paracetamol. A note scribbled on the hotel's headed notepad in an angular, masculine handwriting read, *No more than 4 in 24 hours.*

The ointment, the massage, the tender touch of his fingers had been a doctor's. Her warped mind — convinced that all men must want sex all the time — had made her misread the signs. He wasn't the same kind of man as those she had known in her life. He was one of those rare honest and decent men that she knew existed but had seldom met.

He had insisted on checking her back because he was genuinely concerned for her health, not because he was attracted to her and wished to get his hands on her. He hadn't been about to kiss her when Laura had knocked. She had imagined it.

Wished it.

Well, all the better. She had nothing to offer him. Her dowry was a chip on her shoulder against men that was the size of a boulder and she had a deep-rooted fear of marriage and family.

And Brad had suffered enough. He deserved a woman who could give him everything he needed — a woman with a clean conscience who could convince him that he wasn't guilty of killing his girlfriend. While she, who had killed her own baby, was the last person who could do that. She was the last person who deserved him.

* * * *

At the first notes of the dawn chorus, Brad was awake. Memories of the night before flooded back. For the first time ever, he had been able to talk about the accident without barbed wire coiling in his throat. He had managed to say Frances' name without his voice breaking. But what had happened in the bedroom next... That alone required some deep soul-searching and explaining.

What the hell had he been thinking? If Laura hadn't knocked on the door, he would have kissed Sonia — and a lot more. Judging from the way she had looked at him, they would have gone all the way to a place from which there was no return — not as simple colleagues, in any case. His head instantly filled with the perfect curve of the small of her back, the warmth of her skin and the curls that tumbled out of her bun, brushing the back of his hand. It had been sensory overload. Duty had quickly slipped into pleasure, and professionalism had whooshed down the drain.

When she had turned around and looked at him with those deep, dark eyes — they were branded in his brain, ricocheting in his dreams — things had spun totally out of control. Until that moment, his cold detachment had shielded him from her. But when he read the same desire in her eyes, the dam had broken.

That was why he hadn't stayed up waiting for her but had hidden in his bed, pretending to sleep. He couldn't risk things getting out of control again. After all, it was unlikely that another child would knock on their door and rescue them in the nick of time.

He'd have to be a lot more careful now that things had slipped between them. It would be so easy to fall in love with Sonia, but he had nothing to offer her other than guilt, regret and nightmares.

The first rays of dawn illuminated the wisteria clusters, burning the dew off the stone banister. It was going to be a hot day.

When Sonia opened the French doors, wearing a floaty, flowery dress, she looked like a vision from Botticelli's painting *Spring*.

"Thanks for the pills," she said.

"How is your back? And Charlotte?"

"Both are fine. Charlotte was doing a little stargazing in the hotel garden. I'm off to wake the kids now. You can use the room. See you downstairs for breakfast."

She sounded pleasant but a little distant. Maybe she too regretted what had happened between them the night before.

As soon as she was gone, Brad dialed the concierge to remind them about his room.

"Sure, Mr. Wilson. A few guests are checking out this morning, so you will definitely get your own room tonight."

Then he got himself ready for a shower, but not before engaging the latch on the suite's door. *I'm not running any risks this time.*

His gaze fell on the words printed on the zipped plastic bag where he kept his toiletries. *Once thawed, content cannot be refrozen.* A chill ran through him. What if the same applied to his relationship with Sonia?

Chapter Eight

Sonia had dreaded the visit to the Capuchin friars' catacombs from the moment the idea had been floated by the history department. For centuries, the Capuchin friars had embalmed the bodies of their dead and those of paying customers. By the time they'd stopped embalming, in 1920, they had amassed a veritable collection of cadavers in period clothes in all states of preservation from skeletons to plump-cheeked mummies. The history teachers had tasked the kids with comparing the friars' embalming methods with those of the ancient Egyptians. Although spending a morning surrounded by thousands of corpses wasn't Sonia's idea of fun, her history colleagues had insisted that it was necessary.

Now that they were assembled outside the drab and dusty monastery, she was even more convinced that coming here had been a mistake. A good many students would find it distressing, disturbing or gross. Those who didn't would be tormenting the others.

At least Brad didn't look at all perturbed. In fact, he looked particularly handsome in his dark green T-shirt that matched the color of his eyes. Or maybe it was the way the sun shone on his mussed hair, making it shimmer with warm, coppery sparkles.

He turned abruptly and caught her looking at him, so she hurried to justify herself by asking him a question. "Are you still okay with dealing with the 'casualties' while I look after the rest?" She would have much rather been the one taking the students out, but Brad's medical training meant that it made more sense for him to deal with people who felt unwell.

"Sure. I'll meet you here." He pointed to a set of steps bathed by sunlight. They were the entrance to the cemetery where, presumably, they buried the people who didn't care or have the money to be made eternal with formalin. It was a beautiful garden, with white marble statues and tidy evergreens.

My baby wasn't buried. She chased the thought away.

Not a moment too late, a portly friar welcomed them cheerfully in heavily accented English. He led them into a warren of corridors lined with skeletons wrapped in papery skin and old rags in all the possible shades of dust. Every now and then, a velvet jacket, a monk's habit or a priest's vestment suggested something about the life of the person who had once inhabited the body.

The whole time, Sonia scanned the children for sudden pallor or a telltale swaying but, judging by their exclamations of "Wow!", "Creepy!", "Handsome!", they weren't much fazed by the macabre sights. Still, it was important to catch swooners before they hit the ground, as faintings were quickly recoverable, but the injuries from dropping like lead to the floor weren't always so.

Their tour leader's healthy chubbiness, his bouncy step and his chirpy voice were somewhat at odds with the somberness of that industrial-scale sepulcher. *At least* he *is enjoying himself.*

"Miss, do you believe in ghosts?" Charlotte had sidled up to her and she was darting her eyes left to right, as if she expected a skeleton to suddenly jump out at her like in a scary fairground ride.

"No, Charlotte. But if you're afraid, you can stick with me and I'll beat off any specters that make advances on you." Sonia smiled and saw Charlotte's face relax into a germ of a smile.

"And now our *pezzo forte*, the highlight! Our *bella addormentata*, our sleeping beauty!" the friar piped.

He led them to a beautiful glass coffin where a perfectly preserved toddler with a yellow ribbon in her hair seemed asleep. Her cheeks were still plump and her eyelids were a little open, as if she might wake up at any moment.

Memories of her dead baby girl exploded in Sonia's mind like a nail bomb. This time, she could not push them away. Her breaths became quick and shallow and an invisible vise clamped her chest and throat. This was going to be a whopper of an asthma attack.

Instead of doing the logical thing—reaching for her inhaler—Sonia shot a panicked look to Brad and found him already watching her.

He whispered something in Jake's ear, squeezed through the group and reached her. "Where's your inhaler?"

She rummaged in her bag and plugged it into her mouth, squeezing the canister. Meanwhile, he slipped his arm around her waist and steered her toward the exit. There was bright sunshine outside, and Sonia felt like she had emerged from Polyphemus' cave.

A few more puffs, together with the clean air and the distraction of the kaleidoscopic displays of the flower sellers, eventually released Sonia's bronchi from their spasm. Brad helped her sit on the steps—the ones where they'd agreed to meet if he had to take kids out—and didn't take his eyes off her for a moment. Tender concern furrowed his brow, but she felt safe now.

Maybe it was the sun's warmth on her skin and the stone steps that felt hot under her legs… *Life is warm. Death is cold*. Or maybe it was Brad's presence. Was it because he was a doctor that she felt safe, contained, like a flailing child held tight so that she couldn't hurt herself or others? Or was it something else about him? There wasn't a drop of hurry or of *I'm-wasting-my-time* about the way he sat by her with his elbows on his knees, his head turned to her and the most tender look in his eyes. Everything about him said, *I'm staying here for as long as you need me*.

In her experience, men didn't stay. The father of her baby had bolted at the first mention of her pregnancy. *Don't think about the baby. That's how you got the asthma attack.*

"I'm sorry. This isn't how it was supposed to go. You shouldn't have had to take *me* out," she said.

"You warned me that you might faint. But having an asthma attack instead of fainting? That's cheating."

Lovely creases fanned from his eyes as he smiled—and did strange things to Sonia's insides.

"Take another puff if you need to."

"I'm all right, thanks. We can go back in."

He shook his head, clicking his tongue. "Not yet. That place is a cave of dust."

It wasn't the dust. "I can't leave the children."

"They're with Jake and Katie, and I've told Jake that I was taking you out."

"But I must go back for the workshop."

"That's out of the question. The formalin's vapors will trigger another attack."

"Is this Brad the doctor speaking, or…" What could she call him? The way he had looked after her, jumping to her every need, wasn't something to be expected from a colleague. He had massaged her wrists on the airplane, paid for the suite and offered it to her, taken the sofa when he was forced to seek her hospitality and rubbed balm on her bruises, for which he had chased, punched and sworn at her attacker. And now he had rushed her out and was sitting by her with no apparent intention to leave. "The friend?"

He shifted his gaze. "Which of the two would find you more compliant?"

Cheeky. He had turned the question back to her. "Look, Brad… I'll be fine. It wasn't the dust that caused the attack. Or, at least, it only partly did."

He was silent, neither asking nor stopping her from telling him what had caused it. Sonia appreciated that delicate, considerate silence. But, for the first time in years, she felt that she wanted to tell someone. "Seeing the dead girl brought back some difficult memories."

"I'm sorry."

"You couldn't have known. The dust was the most obvious culprit."

"I'm not sorry about the misdiagnosis. I'm sorry that you lost someone."

It was the first time anyone had called her baby 'someone'. For everyone else, that fetus had been a 'pregnancy'—an 'it'. Tears welled in her eyes and, without looking, Brad sensed them and wrapped his arm around her shoulders. That sympathetic gesture summoned more tears, until big fat drops were chasing each other down her cheeks.

"I didn't *lose* someone, Brad. I *killed* someone." The words tumbled out of her mouth, and, now that the dam was broken, there was no way to stop the water from gushing out. "I got pregnant at sixteen. My parents are old-fashioned Sicilians. They reacted very badly and pressured me into having an abortion. Twelve years haven't been enough to forget." She shuddered.

"You can't blame yourself. You were only sixteen."

"It's not blame, Brad. It's...raw, stinging regret. I've missed that baby from the moment I knew she was being taken away from me. When I look at our students, I think that my child could have been one of them. And when I see a dead baby or a dead child..." She burst into sobs and he squeezed her shoulders.

"Where was the baby's father in all this?" There was reproach in his voice.

"He disappeared as soon as I told him that I was pregnant. To be fair, he was sixteen too." She pulled a tissue out of her bag and wiped her eyes and nose. "I'm sorry. I shouldn't be blubbering—"

"Don't be. I sure know what it's like to live with grief and regret. The only people who don't cry anymore are those over there." He gestured to the graves beyond the stone wall.

"But it's unprofessional to blubber away while I should be on duty, on the shoulder of..." Earlier, he

113

hadn't confirmed that she could call him a friend, so she played it safe. "A colleague."

"Yes, I'm so unfit as a shoulder to cry on that I haven't even brought a packet of tissues." The corners of his lips curled up.

A sound between a sob and a laugh burst out of her and she threw her arms around him. "Oh, Brad, you're—"

But his body tensed under her touch and she immediately let go of him.

"I'm what?" A blush had spread across his cheeks.

"You're…something special."

Sonia leaned back, resting her elbows on the step behind, closed her eyes and tossed her head back. The warmth of the sun on her neck, Brad's comforting presence— "Oh, no, I forgot!" She whipped back up to sitting. "I was meant to stand by Charlotte and beat the ghosts away."

Brad cocked an eyebrow and smiled. "Ghosts can't be *beaten* away, Sonia. They're immaterial. Then again, maybe I'm not the only one who's 'special' around here."

Seeing Sonia gasping for air, he'd felt like the catacombs' walls were closing in on him and burying him alive—as if his own lungs had been thirsting for oxygen.

He had experienced something like this when he'd discovered that Frances hadn't survived. But hers had been a disproportionate reaction for a colleague suffering a mild asthma attack. He had seen people in much worse physical distress during his overseas volunteering, even after the accident, but none of them had triggered that kind of reaction. Was his PTSD regressing or…? The other possibility didn't bear thinking about.

Sonia insisted on rejoining the others but, all through the embalming workshop, he kept a hawk's eye on her, on maximum alert for the first signs of another attack. Should he need to sweep her off her feet and whisk her out of the building against her will, he'd do it.

Poor girl. What she must have gone through at only sixteen. At least his tragedy had struck him when he had been a full-grown man. It had left him brittle and cracked, but perhaps one day the cracks might be plastered over. Twelve years was a long time for her to bear the scars of her trauma. He sincerely hoped that she could put it all behind her one day and be happy, perhaps find a man who deserved her—even if that thought gave him goosebumps of jealousy.

When they finally emerged from the dingy, grim corridors into the blazing sunshine outside, it almost felt like a resurrection. But he wouldn't stop watching over her. Even if he decided to stop—and he *had* tried— there wouldn't be a moment when he wasn't aware of her. He couldn't be in the same room as her without feeling a buzz of electricity, a magnetic pull, a gravitational force. And when she was elsewhere, his thoughts were still with her.

He had battled this ridiculous sense of connection with her when she had joined the school. He had tried to keep her at a distance, but he'd had as little success as if the earth had decided to spin away from the sun. He was now fully inside her orbit and he feared that, like the earth would eventually spiral into the sun, so he would spiral into her, burning to ashes in the process.

After an abundant lunch in an earthy trattoria, they climbed back onto their coach to reach Mondello beach, just outside Palermo. Brad was about to sit in his usual place, away from Sonia, when it hit him how ridiculous and rude it would be, after sharing their pasts' most painful secrets.

He caught a flicker of surprise in her face as he sat on the seat next to hers and felt the need to justify himself. "I must keep an eye on my patient."

Her jaw twitched. Maybe she didn't like to be considered his patient, like he didn't like to think of himself as her doctor.

"Tell me something." She turned her body to face him. "How come you were free to come on this trip? Shouldn't you be volunteering somewhere with Doctors Without Borders?"

"I should be, but there was a problem with my visa, so I couldn't go."

"Ah. What a wonderful piece of luck." She rushed to add, "For the kids. The trip couldn't have gone ahead without you and they would have been very disappointed. Thank you."

"My pleasure."

"It isn't, really. And you never lie, remember?"

She hadn't missed a beat, but she was wrong. "I'm enjoying this trip, actually."

She smiled with surprise. "I'm glad." A beat, then, "What have you enjoyed most?"

You. "Sicily's beauty."

Her left eyebrow kicked up. "You are going to see a lot of 'beauty' *and* 'beauties' at the beach this afternoon, I'm sure," she teased.

"I'm sure I will." *Because you'll be there.*

"And I think you'll like Etna very much. I must warn you, though… We won't find any bubbling lava."

"It's fine." Why should he care about Etna's lava when his own blood turned lava-like every time she was near him? *Stop thinking about her this way.*

The sun, filtering through the coach's enormous tinted window, played wonderful games with her hair and with the color of her skin and her clothes. She hadn't changed a bit since the day she'd walked into the school's drab staffroom and set it alight with life and color. *She's no less dangerous.*

"Look, the sea!" she exclaimed with childish excitement.

They had emerged from a forested area and were gliding down a dual carriageway with a strip of blooming oleander running down the middle. In the distance, a tongue of sapphire sea glittered in the sun. It wasn't one sparkle less beautiful than the seas of the Philippines, Hawaii or Maldives he had loved. And the Sicilian sun had turned the world to full technicolor. The more he saw of Sicily, the more he was falling in love with it. *And with a certain young Sicilian lady.*

No, he wasn't falling in love with Sonia. Yes, they had moved on beyond a solely professional relationship, but it was just friendship. She'd said it herself when she asked him if he was speaking as a doctor or as a friend. He could perfectly well handle being friends with her. *You're deluding yourself.* It would be a shame *not* to be friends after the way they had opened up to each other, sharing the most painful memories of their pasts without hesitation, without shame — easily, as if they had always been meant to.

"At this time of year, Mondello is at its best. The season hasn't started, so the beach huts haven't been put up yet," she said.

"That's good. The boys have set their minds on a football match."

"And there I was, imagining that they'd be pawing the sand to jump into the water just because that's what I used to do as a child."

"Maybe you didn't like football."

Sonia cracked a smile. "Anyway, it's better if they play football rather than dive into the water with a full stomach. The driver warned me that the sea is very cold this time of year, but I doubt he has any idea of how cold Atlantic beaches are."

"Quite. I remember holidaying with my parents in Cornwall and my skin turning blue like a Smurf's as soon as I touched the water."

He couldn't imagine Sonia's warm, dark skin turning blue, but he could easily — joyfully — imagine her in a bikini, swimming like a mermaid. Would her curls stretch and soften in the water or would they remain springy and bouncy? *Stop thinking about her.*

"I can't imagine you as a child," she said thoughtfully.

"I didn't leap out of the head of Zeus fully adult and fully armed."

"I never thought of you as the god of war." She stretched her back against the seat rest. "What kind of child were you?"

"A quiet one. I liked my own company."

"I could have guessed." The edges of her lips curved in a smile. "And what did you want to be as a grown-up?"

"An explorer."

"That's fitting for a lone wolf." She thought a little. "When did you think of becoming a doctor?"

"When I heard about Doctors Without Borders."

"And, of course, you chose to be a surgeon rather than a GP so that the people you'd be interacting with would be mostly unconscious."

He smiled. "I suppose so. Now tell me about you." He didn't need to ask her what kind of child she'd been. He could easily imagine her. She was one of those lucky people who had retained their childhood's curiosity, optimism and sense of wonder. "For example, what did you want to be when you were a child?"

"Anything but a housewife like my mother." A shadow clouded her eyes. "In my late teens, I decided that I wanted to be a secondary school teacher so that I could be there for my students when they need someone outside their families to help them…" Her voice trailed off.

Brad didn't need an explanation. He could guess at what time in her life she had wished that adults other than her parents had been available and supportive. And he longed to have been there for her. "You're doing a wonderful job at it."

"Not really. Not on this trip."

* * * *

The coach stopped a few meters from a beach as golden as Sonia remembered it. Everyone tumbled out of the vehicle like bouncy marbles, but their excitement was nothing compared to that of the street sellers who had been idling on an otherwise-empty beach. The five dark-skinned men ran with their trolleys and boards that were tingling with necklaces, sunglasses and beach paraphernalia.

"Aha! We need a football," Jake said, and started inspecting the crowded display of a grinning seller. The amount of stuff the man lugged about single-handedly was phenomenal, and the way he balanced about a dozen hats piled on top of each other onto his head was nothing short of a juggler's act.

"And we could do with some *tamburello* rackets," Sonia said, reaching for her wallet.

"What's *tamburello*?" Charlotte asked.

"An Italian beach game, a bit like tennis but without bouncing the ball off the ground. I'll teach you."

"Oh, floating mattresses!" Katie exclaimed. "Can you ask him if he has a double one?"

Some of the girls bought some necklaces and earrings, despite Sonia pointing out that they were not needed at the beach and there was plenty of similar stuff in shops back in town. Laura and Hazel argued over how they should share the five-for-three-euros offer on the fridge magnets. Lucy timidly purchased a bucket-and-spade set and asked for a non-see-through bag. Ryan bought a very large inflatable turtle with an exaggerated grin, paying no attention to the other boys taunting him. Brad asked for some sun lotion, causing much consternation and confabulation among the very dark-skinned sellers.

Sonia came to his rescue. "You can use mine," she offered. Then Sonia remembered when she had been packing for the trip and imagined herself having a secret giggle when Brad turned up to the beach unprepared because he had refused to listen to the plans. How things had changed! She scanned the sellers' display and was relieved to see that they also had a few pair of swimming trunks, should Brad need them. But where would he get changed? She pictured him changing under a towel and the image of him wrapped in just a towel, straight out of the shower, flashed across her mind and warmed her cheeks.

As soon as Jake kicked off the football match, all the boys abandoned the sellers and the girls followed soon. T-shirts flew off their backs and their shorts were kicked off milky-white legs.

"No kicking sand and no getting in the water until we tell you," Sonia called out.

"Yes, Miss," Aidan shouted, already running after Jake's football.

Then Brad tugged his T-shirt over his head — two hands behind his neck, the way men did — and Sonia lost control of her eyes. The good news was that he had packed a pair of swimming trunks and he was wearing them. The bad news was that, even with his trunks on, there were was just too much man. Rays of sun chiseled his body, highlighting every glorious muscle with a chiaroscuro of shadows and light. He was hotter than the Sicilian sun.

When she had walked in on him having a shower, it hadn't been proper to let her eyes linger, but now it was okay to enjoy the sight, so long as she didn't make it too obvious. *Stop gawping.*

Watching wasn't quite enough, though. She ached to reach out and run her hands over the bumps of his chest, his arms, his thighs. Did they feel as rock-solid as they looked? *This is utterly unprofessional.* Anyway, she was done with men.

Wasn't she?

Well…if a thoroughly lovely and decent man like Brad were available… *He's not available…not to me anyway.*

"Did you say that you could lend me some sun lotion?" He suddenly looked at her and caught her staring.

"Yes, yes, of course." She rummaged inside her bag, grateful of an excuse to hide her face, and pulled out a bottle of factor twenty. "It's not very strong, so you'll have to slather it on quite generously. I'm a little darker than you." *Duh.*

"Thanks." He took the bottle, squeezed it onto his hands and started spreading it on his face with the palms of his hands. Then he rubbed it onto on his chest and shoulders and Sonia's knees wobbled a little. Damn, she should find something else to do while she waited for the bottle back, instead of gawping at him.

But as she saw him struggle to reach his back, she couldn't help herself. "Would you like me to spread it on your back?" *You just want to feel the guy up, don't you?*

He hesitated for a moment — long enough to make Sonia totally regret what she'd said and feel like a dirty perv — then smiled and offered her the bottle. "Thank you."

Sonia swallowed. She would use her palms, not the tips of her fingers, because people didn't touch with palms, they touched with fingers. Palms were safe. Flat palms. *Here we go.* She squirted the cream onto the palm of her right hand and slapped it right in the middle of Brad's back. But as soon as her hand made contact with his skin, her palms softened, her fingers curled and her whole arm tingled with sensation as she ran over the ridges of his muscles until she felt like the sand was shifting under her and she had to dig her feet deeper to stop herself toppling over. There was so much of him that she had to squeeze more cream onto her hand. And the answer to her previous question was yes, his muscles felt as hard as they looked.

As she dropped her dress into a pile on the sand, exposing her body in all its bikini-clad glory, he had to run a hand over his face to keep himself together. How was he ever going to be friends with…so much woman? This small Sicilian lady did things to his internal chemistry that were not within the realms of friendship. He was mighty glad that he was wearing loose swimming shorts instead of tight Speedos. The friendship utopia tumbled off its plinth like a dictator's statue pulled down by a mob.

Even though it wasn't good for him, he couldn't take his eyes off her glossy skin, her shiny black locks and her generous body. She matched the landscape like a missing piece. She was distilled sunshine, roaring sea and golden sand. On that first day in the school, she had flooded the staffroom with sunshine because she *was* sunshine.

"Mr. Wilson, pass?" Jake shouted, kicking the football at him.

He caught it then kicked it back and joined the game, grateful of the distraction. But, even then, he couldn't help shooting surreptitious glances at Sonia playing *tamburello* with Charlotte. While she chased the ball with the tambourine-shaped racket, her curls bounced on her shoulders as if they had a life of their own, mesmerizing him.

"Mr. Wilson, that ball was for you," one of the boys complained when he missed it.

"Sorry." He must pay more attention.

Jake shot him a knowing look, then called half-time. "Mr. Wilson is so unfit that he needs a rest," he teased.

"I wish I was that unfit," Aidan shouted, and everyone laughed.

"Can we swim now?" Ryan asked.

"He just wants to cuddle up to his turtle," Jonathan called, and everyone laughed again.

"Right… No turtle ride for you," Ryan replied, mock-offended. "Can we swim, Mr. Wilson?"

"Let's check with Miss Alletti," Brad said.

She had stopped playing *tamburello* and was sitting on her towel on the sand next to Charlotte and Laura. While Ryan and his friends raced to grab the turtle, Brad walked up to Sonia. From his standing position, all he could see was a cascade of curls and her lovely, lovely cleavage. He immediately tore his eyes away and dug his toes into the hot sand as punishment. This trip to the beach would never be over early enough. She looked up.

Concentrate on her face.

"Miss Alletti, the children wonder if they can swim now."

"What do you think, Mr. Wilson?" The sun made her squint and curl her nose cutely.

"It should be okay now."

"Why can't we swim on a full tummy?" Charlotte asked.

"You can work it out by yourself. I'll give you a clue. There's a risk of drowning because of competition between two organ systems in the body," Brad said.

"The digestive system?"

"Yes. And what else?"

"I don't know. I give up."

"Muscles?" Laura suggested.

"Correct. And what do both the muscles and the digestive organs need to function?"

"Oxygen?" Charlotte volunteered.

"You're getting there. And how is oxygen transported?"

"In the blood! They're competing for blood?"

Brad loved seeing Charlotte's eyes light up with the excitement of having got to the answer. "And when muscles don't get enough blood, they cramp."

He could feel Sonia's gaze on him and Charlotte. It was a benevolent gaze, like that of a mother. Perhaps he was wrong, but Sonia seemed to have a special attachment to this girl. The night before, when she had been missing, Sonia had insisted on going looking for her herself.

"But you should be fine by now, so Miss Alletti says that you can swim," he finished, and Charlotte and Laura ran to tell the others.

Ryan's group hurled the turtle into the water and jumped on it, trying to push each other off at the first opportunity. Katie launched herself onto her inflatable mattress while Jake called, "Race to the pontoon?" and a sand cloud lifted as all the children ran to the water.

Sonia shifted sideways on the towel and patted the space next to her. "Have a seat, if you'd like. It seems that Jake and Katie are entertaining the children for us."

"Thanks." He sat down next to her and their legs brushed, sending a surge of electricity through his body. "They seem to be really gelling with the kids."

"Jake is a natural with children. I've noticed it at school too. Some chefs hide in the kitchen, but he's often out and about, checking to find out how the kids like his food." She turned to face him. "And you're simply great with the children."

125

It was one of the best compliments she could have paid him. "What makes you think that?"

"The way you made Charlotte come up with the answer by herself instead of spoon-feeding her the facts. And anyone can see that the children love you to bits, even when you get distracted and miss a ball." Her toes curled in the sand. Did she have an inkling that she'd been the reason for his distraction? The awkward silence that followed suggested that it might be the case, and he looked down at his half-buried feet.

"Do you ever miss being a surgeon?" she asked.

"I don't give myself the chance to think about it."

"Why?"

"It would be of no benefit to know the answer. I'm never going back to it."

"You can't punish yourself forever, Brad. Even if you insist on blaming yourself for the accident, every penance in this world comes to an end eventually."

The sloshing of the waves, the cries of the seagulls and the cries of the children in the water filled the silence between them.

"But I'm glad you don't want to leave teaching. It would be a great loss for the children if you left the school" — she hesitated — "and not just for them…"

Her last words trailed off, but Brad heard them and his heart gave a little somersault.

"How's your back?" Not that he had checked it over and over from the moment she had slipped out of her dress. All right, he'd seen that the bruise was still there, but he didn't know if it still hurt.

"Much better, thank you." A shy smile flashed across her face before she looked away. Was she thinking about the back massage that had been well on the way to turning into something more?

"Mr. Wilson! Miss Alletti! Come! Everyone is swimming to the platform," Charlotte called from the water.

"Leave them be, Charlotte. They haven't digested their big, greedy lunches yet," Jake shouted.

Brad felt something warm and fuzzy in his chest. Jake and Katie were clearly trying to play matchmaker between him and Sonia. There was nothing particularly unusual there. What surprised him was that it didn't bother him at all.

"We can't laze around here while everyone is having fun. Race you to the water?" Sonia leaped up, grabbing his hand. A frisson of electricity crackled through that contact, but it only lasted a second, because she immediately let go and ran.

He chased after her but not so fast as to catch up. He'd rather admire her from a distance. *Much safer.*

She dived headfirst into the water, sleek like a needle. As she swam butterfly-style, her arms opened like wings and droplets trailed behind, forming a shimmering lace of water. He'd rather wade in until he could no longer touch the bottom or doggy paddle all the way to the platform than swim and take his eyes off her. She could have been born from the foam of the sea like Aphrodite. She was a pearl, now reunited with her oyster.

Ahead, the kids were churning the sea into a frantic foam.

"Come on, Mr. Wilson!" Sonia called when she turned and caught him still near the shore.

Even from a distance, her lips shone glossy red like sea anemones and her wet curls hung springy and coiled like the tendrils of a sweet-pea plant. Just watching her swim and have fun made his heart melt.

'Colleagues' was a joke. 'Friends' wasn't enough. He wanted more. He wanted her all.

He took a breath in, aimed at the transparent turquoise water and dove in headfirst — in every way.

Chapter Nine

The shock of the cold sea had momentarily cooled her head, but it only lasted until she saw Brad's elegant front-crawl strokes, his hair darkened by the water and wet eyelashes framing eyes of liquid turquoise. As he shook his head out of the water and smiled, he wedged himself firmly back in hers. Sonia switched from butterfly to front crawl and leaped ahead as fast as she could, not out of competitiveness but in a vain attempt to break free of his gravity.

Tugged in all directions, the turtle was still some way from the platform when Ryan leaped off and swam ahead, reaching the platform first. "I win!" he shouted.

Jake had made sure to arrive a little after and, in a flurry of splashes, the platform filled with panting, shoving, giggling kids, under Jake and Katie's watchful eyes. Some dove gracefully back into the water, others bombed in, a few were pushed with peals of laughter.

Last, the turtle was heaved up too. "The Ninja Turtle has made it!" Jonathan shouted.

Brad reached the platform before Sonia and, with a powerful push of his lower back and a tug of his biceps, he heaved his long body onto it. Drops of sea water ran down his chest and arms, glistening in the sun. If sea gods existed, they must look just like that.

"Watch me dive, Mr. Wilson," Aidan called, before leaping headfirst into the water.

Brad complimented him and advised on possible improvements. *He'd make a wonderful father.* Sonia chased the thought away. If, one day, Brad was going to be a father — and she wished that for him, sincerely — it certainly wouldn't be with her. She wasn't worthy of being a mother. Her chance had come — too early, unfortunately — and she had pushed it away. She didn't deserve another one. She certainly didn't deserve Brad.

"May I give you a hand up, Miss Alletti?" he offered, stretching out his arm. There were dimples on his cheeks and a smile in every way as tender as the ones he reserved for the children. It instantly warmed the sea.

She didn't check whether her bikini was still covering all the places it needed to, as she always did before getting out of the water, and she didn't care that she could easily clamber onto the platform under her own steam. She gripped his forearm and let him grip hers and pull her up.

"Someone is sinking this platform," Jake called out playfully. "It's Mr. Wilson and Miss Alletti! They're too heavy!"

"No, they're not. They're very slim!" Charlotte protested. "It's the turtle."

"Abandon ship!" Jake pressed on.

Ryan launched the turtle off the platform and jumped, almost bursting it. Aidan shot a glance at Brad to check if he was looking, then dived elegantly headfirst. Jonathan dive-bombed, while Tracey squealed when she was hit by the spray, as if she hadn't just come out of the water. Then everyone else leaped off at once, rocking the platform like an earthquake.

"Let's play water polo," Jake suggested.

"You can use the floating mattresses for the goals," Katie offered, and everyone started swimming back to the shore, turtle included, in a flurry of kicks and spray.

When the shockwaves subsided, Sonia found herself alone on the platform with Brad. Jake and Katie were so obviously trying to get them together that it was almost sweet. It was especially touching that they considered her a good enough match for Brad. That thought tickled a place deep in her heart where hopes and dreams still roamed.

Jake and Katie don't know about my baby.

Brad was leaning back on his elbows, one knee bent, eyes closed, looking happy, relaxed and gorgeous.

Too gorgeous for me.

The others had reached the shallows now and were about to start the game.

"Mr. Wilson, come and play?" Aidan called.

A pained look flashed across Brad's face as he opened his eyes and sat up.

Please, go. No, stay.

He hesitated, then shouted back, "The next game." His deep voice echoed off the mountain guarding the bay, the way it only happens at sea, and resonated in her chest. He wasn't going. He was staying. Sonia's heart beat faster.

"Everyone wants a piece of you." It was a comment meant to defuse the electricity sizzling between them but, unfortunately, it was well and truly a Freudian slip.

"Who does?" He pinned her with his jade-green eyes. Sparks of mischief and desire danced in them, making her heart twang. Maybe, the night before, when he had massaged the ointment onto her bruises, his touch *hadn't* been that of a doctor. Maybe she *hadn't* misread his hungry gaze. Maybe he *had* ached to kiss her as much as she had ached to kiss him.

She broke eye contact, trying to calm down the shoal of flying fish trapped in her belly, trying to think of an answer that wasn't the truth.

Swim away.

She hugged her legs as if she was straitjacketing her wayward body, preventatively. The seagull screeched a strident warning and the sea glittered invitingly.

Swim off.

But her legs wouldn't take her off that blasted platform. She couldn't resist looking up and into his eyes.

And she saw it, his gaze caressing her lips. It was a gaze that told her, without any reasonable doubt, that he wanted her as much as she wanted him.

Dangerous knowledge.

It told her that he would make love to her then and there, on that floating platform in the middle of the sea under the watching sun.

And the scariest thing was that she wouldn't have minded.

In fact, she wanted it. If he only so much as scooped her into his arms, the last crumbs of sense in her skull would dissolve like salt in water. And things between them would never be the same again.

Swim away.

"I'm hot," she croaked, and rolled into the water as urgently and ungracefully as a seal chased by a sea lion. It was a ridiculously escape.

Sensible. Cowardly. *Unavoidable.*

She swam down and down, the cold water sizzling against her hot skin, as far away as she could from the eyes that had caused havoc inside her. Her ears popped but she continued to swim down into the calm green belly of the sea — the only place where she could find peace.

She reached the meadow of blooming seagrass with its slender leaves swaying in the current with its olive-like fruits. The current exposed a flash of red among the leaves. A starfish. Sonia swam until she could stroke its velvety legs. Then she flipped around and admired the shimmering bubbles trailing upward behind her and the beams of sunlight scattered by the undulating surface of the water. It was beautiful.

But the dark shadow of the platform was so small, so distant! Primeval panic flooded her nerves.

I can't make it back.

Suddenly a vise clamped around her chest. Her heart rate shot up. She hungered for air. Eyes trained to the surface, she swam upward, but her body demanded air. Another shadow appeared by the platform, then a muffled sound and a shimmer of bubbles…Brad diving in.

With his arms stretched out in front, he weaved through the water with powerful strokes. He reached her, wrapped an arm around her waist and inverted his course to swim back to the surface.

Down there, in the womb of the sea, where the rules of the land didn't apply, they weren't colleagues or teachers or desperately unsuitable lovers — just two human beings clinging to life. But Sonia couldn't last. Her head had started spinning, her ears ringing and her grip on Brad's shoulders slackened. In her daze and confusion, she barely realized what was happening when he sealed his lips around her mouth and shared his air.

When they bobbed out of the water, gasping and spluttering, he was still holding her to his chest. A new dizziness spun Sonia's head, which had nothing to do with lack of oxygen and all to do with being wrapped in Brad's arms.

He hooked one arm onto the platform and slowed down the thrust of his legs. The sun reflecting off the water's surface played amazing tricks in those green irises, which were searching deeply into hers. "Are you all right?"

She didn't know. Between the panic, the fainting and the fireworks that had exploded in her head the moment his lips had touched hers, she had lost most of her cognitive abilities. All she knew was that his body was pressed against hers, their legs intertwined, kicking to stay afloat. And she could feel his lovely warmth. They were alone, hidden from the shore by twenty inches of platform sticking out of the water. Their breaths had synced, their chests heaved together, her breasts pushed against his chest every time they took in air. Lovely air.

But his eyes were dark with worry.

She wanted to tell him that she was all right, to thank him for being there again for her when she needed him. But her throat was thick with emotion.

So she did the only thing that she could, the only thing that felt natural, the thing that her body was screaming for. Floating in the water, their height difference was obliterated, and Sonia didn't have any trouble reaching his lips — and kissing him.

It took her a couple of moments to notice that he wasn't kissing her back.

Oh God, what have I done?

He had given her mouth-to-mouth resuscitation and she had mistaken it for a kiss! He had rescued her from drowning, and she thanked him by sexually assaulting him!

Panicking, she pulled away, but he tightened his arm around her. His expression was torn. Tortured. Then a low growl emerged from some primeval place deep inside him, and he pressed his lips onto hers — urgently, hungrily, with the desperation of a man who's seen his woman almost die.

But I'm not his woman.

Sonia's body melted against his as he pulled her closer. Between them was only a little Lycra and a substantial erection.

She parted her lips and their tongues became intertwined like their legs. If her body dissolved into his like salt into seawater, Sonia wouldn't have been surprised — nor would she have minded. She wrapped her arms around Brad's neck in joyful abandon.

Released from the task of holding her afloat, Brad slipped his hand from her waist to her right buttock, cupping and stroking, then he caressed all the way back up to the nape of her neck, sending tingling waves of delicious sensations through her nerves. But it was when he cupped her breast that her breath snagged in her throat, making her gasp for more.

"Mr. Wilson, Miss Alletti! Come and play with us?" the kids called from the shore.

They pulled away from each other like magnets suddenly reversed.

God, what are we doing?

"We must go back," he rasped, avoiding her gaze.

"Yes, we must," she said, stunned and confused.

Without waiting for her, he started swimming back. By tacit agreement, she hung back, so as to avoid them returning to the shore together.

* * * *

He should have left the platform when the children had called him the first time. That kiss had changed everything. It had catapulted them into a totally new territory, to a land he had no idea how to inhabit. And they'd gotten there on a one-way ticket.

What a terrible shame, after they'd only just gotten a nice friendship going. Now, as far as he could see, 'good friendship' was not one of the options. It was either back to awkwardly avoiding each other in the corridors or full-steam-ahead to lovers. But he had nothing to offer Sonia.

His gaze lingered on her lovely face, her delicious lips, slightly parted as she slept on the coach seat next to his. She looked so peaceful. All her humming energy was asleep too. She must be exhausted after the asthma attack at the catacombs then her near-drowning, for which he suspected he was partly to blame. A flash of fear had flitted across her face before she'd dived into the water. He had asked her questions that had scared her and she had escaped him but had gone too deep.

I pushed her too far.

But she had kissed him afterward. Why? Maybe she'd been scared exactly of that — of what she might do if they stayed there any longer. Oh, didn't he know the feeling?

But he hoped that she didn't regret that kiss, because it had been pure magic. Her happiness had rubbed off onto him just with the touch of her lips. With Sonia in his arms, he had felt emotions that he'd thought he'd never feel again — a happiness so strong that it made his heart ache.

There was a sudden jerk, horns blasting, followed by shouted insults in Italian. He saw a motorbike slip away, giving the coach driver the middle finger. It must have been a near miss. A painful shiver rippled through his skin as horrid memories floated back like an oil slick blackening the sea — memories of Frances and her beautiful life cut short by his incompetence and stupidity. He didn't deserve Sonia. He wasn't worthy to be entrusted with another woman. He hadn't taken good enough care of Frances and he must not be allowed to destroy another innocent woman's life, especially not Sonia's.

He must backtrack, re-establish their distance, apologize. He shouldn't have asked her that question on the platform and he should have let go of her once she was safely out of the water. And he certainly should never, ever have kissed her.

Sonia hadn't meant to fall asleep when she'd closed her eyes on the coach. Brad was sitting next to her but had been engaged in conversation with the children who were sitting across the aisle, and Sonia shad hut her eyes to replay that kiss in her mind.

What did that kiss mean? Was it just physical attraction? He wasn't like the other men she had known. He was caring and devoted. *Devoted to the memory of his dead girlfriend.* One day he might be devoted to her instead. Even if that kiss had only been lust, the way he had looked after her at the catacombs wasn't. She had felt a connection growing between them. Did she wish it could grow more? She wasn't prepared to admit it to herself. *But yes.* And that was why that kiss had felt special. Everything about Brad felt special, even just sitting next to him. Her bliss had been so great that, eventually, she had fallen asleep.

When Brad tapped her on the shoulder to wake her up, she felt like she was emerging from the Cretaceous Period. By the time she had caught up with who she was and where, he had already counted the kids off the coach, instructed everyone to go for a shower and given them an appointment in the restaurant for seven-thirty.

"You can have your shower first. I'll hang around here," she said to him. She'd get a shot of strong coffee from the bar while she waited.

"No need. I'm getting my own room tonight," he said flatly.

It was the coldness in his voice that upset her more than the end of their room sharing. It felt like a flashback to the days when he'd give her the cold shoulder in the corridors.

"I'll go up with you to get my stuff, if that's okay," he went on, avoiding her eyes.

Sonia felt like she had woken up from a happy dream, as if the kiss in the sea had never happened. Or was she living a bad dream now? How could this flint-faced man be the same man who had held her tenderly against his body, shared his air and kissed her with such urgency, as if he had been waiting for that moment for months?

"Of course it's okay, Brad. Are *you* okay?"

"Totally fine." No tenderness, no friendliness, no recognition of any kind on his face.

She felt her anger mounting, her heartbeat racing, her hands growing restless. Was she disappointed that tonight they would not be carrying on from where they'd left off at the platform? If that were the case, she'd been stupid to make that assumption. She should just be happy that Brad could finally sleep in a proper bed. And she had longed to have the suite all to herself and be able to use the bathroom in peace. "Then, by all means, feel free to come up to get your stuff when you'd like," she said as coldly as she could manage.

"Thanks. Will do."

She watched him walk up to reception to get his new key as if he were walking out of her life. *Did I think that he was for me? Silly girl, getting ideas above my station!*

When he turned around with a plastic key card in his hand, his face was dripping with relief. "They've given me room three-twenty. They're not charging us for the suite for the remaining days."

"Good. You keep the suite. I'll take three-twenty." That room must be on the same floor as the kids. She'd be closer to them and be able to keep a better eye on Charlotte.

"No," he said with a frown that suggested that, as a gentleman, he considered her idea preposterous. "*You* stay in the suite."

His tone told her that he would be extremely offended if she insisted, so she squeezed out a smile and a thank you.

They went up in the lift in perfect silence, with their eyes pinned to the electronic floor display.

She should be happy. She would continue to enjoy the suite. The hotel wasn't charging for it and Brad would be on night duty for her. Was there anything to be sad about? He had told her before that he needed his 'daily dose of solitude'. He wasn't running away from her. And even if he was? What claim did she have over him?

She watched him stride into the honeymoon suite, hastily shut his half-unpacked suitcase and carry it out without so much as a glance back or a hint of nostalgia or regret. *Niente*. Nothing. In and out of their room like a needle. And she felt like a pierced cloth.

"Supper is at seven-thirty, right?" was all he said when he was waiting for the lift down.

"Yes," she said in a jolly voice meant to hide her disappointment that only succeeded in sounding fake. Then he was swallowed by the lift and was gone.

Sonia stood on the threshold, unable to make sense of things or shut the door. Was this it? After what had happened in the sea, when they'd locked hands and lips like they'd dissolve in the water if they didn't hold on? A kiss like that was no accident. Rather, it had been a wonderful gift that had befallen them in the wrong place and at the wrong time. Now that they had the chance to repeat it in the privacy of a gorgeous suite looking out onto a sea of perfumed *zagara*, he had bolted.

Because he has more sense than you. A fling is not worth the complications at work.

Sure. But maybe for her it wasn't just a fling.

She clicked the door shut with her back and pressed it hard, then she reached for her phone and called her mum.

Her mother was the last woman Sonia would want to grow into. Her mother was the one person who could have helped her keep her baby and, instead, she had sided with her dad. She was narrow-minded, bigoted and uninformed.

But she was the person who loved her most on the entire planet. She would have given both her kidneys for her daughter.

"*Soniuccia, amore*, how are you? Why didn't you call before? I've waited so long…"

"You could have called me too, Mamma."

"I don't know how to do this video thingy."

Sonia had bought her a smartphone and had tried to teach her to make videocalls, but her mum had refused to learn, insisting that it was too difficult. At the beginning Sonia thought that her problem was laziness but eventually realized that it really was beyond her mother's capabilities. A life spent sieving tomato sauce and scrubbing after a husband and a child had taken a toll on her mother's intellectual nimbleness. Sonia would never let that happen to her. She would never marry a man who would want her to stay at home. That was why she had pledged to keep away from men, just in case. But that resolution had started to wobble.

"I'll show you again next time I'm over."

"When? You haven't come for more than two months." A theatrical sigh underscored her words.

"I've been very busy at work. Why don't *you* come to visit me sometime?"

"You know I can't," her mum said with a hint of irritation. She had unsuccessfully tried to learn to drive and she found bus schedules too complicated for her limited English. So she depended entirely on her husband to take her to places that were beyond her walking radius. Unfortunately, he watched football on the weekends and wouldn't give that up, even to visit his daughter.

"You can come on the coach. I'll meet you at the coach station. You're old enough to travel on your own, Mamma."

"I'm *too* old."

Sonia rolled her eyes, forgetting that she was on videocall.

"You can roll your eyes till you're blind, but you'll find out what varicose veins feel like when you're my age."

No, I won't. I won't stand by the stove all day long till my veins pop.

"Has Dad started helping in the house?" The doctor had ordered her mum to put her feet up at least three times a day, but that required her dad to start lifting a finger at home.

Her mum snorted proudly. "What can he do? He's only a man."

"Possession of testicles is not an impairment in the fulfillment of housework duties."

"Why do you have to be so crude?"

"He's been retired for three months. There is no reason why he shouldn't help at home. When will *you* retire?"

"I'm not going to listen if you're going to be stroppy and difficult about your father."

Sonia took a deep breath. This was not the way she had hoped their conversation would go. "How's Auntie Bettina?"

"She's much better, *grazie a Dio*. I'm sure that's because of your cousin's engagement lifting her spirits." A meaningful pause followed.

"Vittoria has gotten engaged?"

"Yes. Finally."

Sonia wasn't biting the hook. "Please give her my congratulations."

"I will." There was a pause, as her mum was probably thinking of another angle to attack the subject. "It's been such a worry for poor Auntie Bettina. Your cousin is twenty-seven. It was high time she thought of settling."

"Worry about what?" *I know perfectly well. I shouldn't wind up my mother just because I'm upset about Brad.*

"That Vittoria would be left on the shelf," her mum replied earnestly.

"What if that shelf isn't such a bad place after all?"

Irritation knotted her mother's brows. "You're playing with fire, Sonia. If you don't stop being stubborn and proud, you'll end up a spinster. How would you like to die alone?"

Better to die alone than live an entire life in bad company.

"I won't be around when you're old," her mother chided her. "Who will look after you if you don't have children?"

"I already had a child, Mum." That was a forbidden topic, one on which they would never see eye to eye. The few times Sonia had brought it up, their conversation had taken a turn for the worse.

I'm sabotaging this call because I'm unhappy with Brad.

Her mum sighed and rolled her eyes. "You're still thinking about that. You'd better not talk about it too much. Men don't like to marry broken goods."

That did it. Sonia raised her voice. "A girl who's had sex is 'broken goods'? We're out of the Middle Ages, Mamma! I don't know what kind of men you are wishing me to marry, but that's not the kind I would even like to sit down to coffee with! I've got to go. Goodbye!"

Sonia flung the phone onto the bed and sank into a chair, steaming with anger—at her mum and at her herself. *Bad daughter.* What had she gotten out of that call? Her mum was old and stuck in her ways. There was no point in trying to change her mind. Why didn't she just steer clear of her bait about Vittoria's engagement? Now both of them were upset and neither had changed the other's mind.

She picked up the phone to call back, but the time was seven-twenty-five. It was time to go down to dinner. Too bad about her shower.

Some of the kids were already waiting by the restaurant's entrance with Jake and Katie, their hair freshly washed and cheeks sun-kissed. They were giggling, joking, messing about. They looked happy. Wasn't that what the trip was about, as well as learning and opening horizons? She could congratulate herself for giving the children a pleasant and educational trip, and Jake and Katie a honeymoon of sorts. It had been hard going for her, and possibly for Brad too, but if this trip was going into the kids' bank of treasured memories, it would have been worth it.

"*Professoressa! Professoressa!*"

The barman had to call her a few more times before Sonia remembered that that was the way Italians call teachers.

"*Sì?*" she replied.

"Are those girls yours?" he asked her in Italian. He was pointing to Charlotte, Hazel, Laura and Tracey, who were sitting on the couches in the smarter bar lounge.

"Yes, they're mine," Sonia replied, feeling it deeply, especially about Charlotte.

"Under-eighteens are not allowed in the bar lounge. I've told them, but they don't seem to understand me — or want to." His arched brow suggested that he was more inclined to believe the latter.

"I'm sorry. I'll talk to them."

She strode up to the girls, who were huddled together, giggling. They hadn't noticed that she was coming over so they jumped when they saw her and tried to hide a phone.

"Show me that phone."

Reluctantly, Laura handed it over. There were photos of Charlotte and Aidan kissing at the beach. Sonia's stomach flipped. Did that happen while she had been behind the platform with Brad? Weren't Katie and Jake watching the kids? *What if they've gotten up to more than kissing? Please, God, no.* Charlotte was only twelve. *But she's an unhappy girl with a troubled home life.* Charlotte was vulnerable and Sonia should have been watching her more closely. She should have *not* disappeared behind a floating platform with one of the other people who were supposed to be looking after the kids. She shuddered.

Four pairs of eyes watched her with trepidation, waiting for her reaction. If she raised her voice and scolded, it might make her feel better, let out some of the anger at herself, but it would have been hypocritical, when she had probably been kissing Brad at the same time as Charlotte had been kissing Aidan.

Slowly, Sonia handed back the phone. "Boys bring heartache and sorrow. Keep away from them at least until you're old enough to deal with the fallout when things go wrong. Now, please, leave this lounge. You are not allowed here." With that, she made to turn and go away, but her shoes crunched some sand. Beach sand. She turned again and noticed the bikini straps around the girls' necks, their calves still dusted with sand. "You haven't even had your showers yet."

"Neither have you, Miss," Charlotte retorted. It was just a comment, without spite or defiance, but it cut close to the bone. In Sonia's discombobulated mind, that comment about one double standard encompassed all her others—from her closeness to Brad when she had told Charlotte to keep away from boys to her unpleasantness to her mum when she had told Charlotte to be nice to hers—and every other mistake she had made since she had been Charlotte's age.

Cornered, she attacked. Jabbing her fists into her waist, she raised her voice. "You should have gone for your showers instead of laying your sandy bottoms on the hotel's special chamois sofas in the grown-ups-only lounge! Now, get up and go to dinner."

The girls immediately got up and, eyes to the ground, sheepishly filed away, pushing the sand on the floor to the side with their flip-flops. Only Charlotte darted her a resentful glance. It pierced Sonia right through.

By the time they entered the dining room, all the others had already sat down and the only seats left were at Brad's table. The girls rushed to sit together, leaving Sonia the seat next to Brad. As if banqueting with the girls that she had just reproached wasn't uncomfortable enough, she had to also dine with the colleague she had kissed when she wasn't supposed to and who had turned into a block of ice on her. In some cases, eating alone wasn't a bad predicament at all.

"*Liscia o gasata*?" he asked her, holding a bottle of water that he was using to fill all the glasses at the table.

"*Liscia, grazie.*"

"I would have bet that you liked sparkly water, Miss," Charlotte said, while Brad poured the water in her glass. "You are such a sparkly person."

"Thanks, Charlotte. I believe that natural goes better with food."

"How can a person be 'sparkly'? It makes no sense," Ryan said.

"They're sparkly when they're nice. You wouldn't know," Charlotte retorted.

"It's just you girls who like sparkly stuff."

"Are you saying that you don't like Miss?"

Oh, please, couldn't they just pay her no attention and pretend that she wasn't there? Because that was what she was wishing for—to not be there.

"Does anyone know what's for dinner tonight?" Sonia asked as a diversion.

"Fish with gnocchi and *caponata*," Brad replied immediately, perhaps feeling as awkward about the previous conversation as she did.

Please, let the caponata have no capers. Sonia hated capers. She was by no means a fussy eater, but capers were her nemesis. Was it because, as a child, she had been forced to stare at a plate of pasta with capers until sunset because she wouldn't eat it? Or was it because they were mushy, pond-green and foul-tasting? It must be the latter.

"I don't like fish," Ryan announced.

"You must at least try it," Brad said.

"I've tried it before."

"Fish are all different, and this one is Sicilian."

"What if a fish bone gets stuck in my throat?"

"If it does, I'll pull it out for you."

"It'll hurt."

"Not a lot. You can't not try the Sicilian fish — or the caponata," Brad said.

Please, God, don't let the caponata have capers. I can't try a caper.

Of course, the caponata had capers. So long as Ryan distracted them by making a scene of every mouthful of fish with gagging sounds and eye-rolls, nobody noticed that Sonia was picking the capers out of the caponata, as if they were poison.

"This is the mouthful that's going to kill me," Ryan recited, stabbing more fish into his fork and guzzling it down. His plate was almost empty.

"It's not going to kill you. It'll only turn you into a turtle," Aidan teased and everyone laughed, much to Ryan's delight, who seemed to love being the center of attention. But once he had cleaned his plate, he was still very much alive and hadn't yet thought of his next comedic sketch, so the others' interest in his antics wavered. Aidan noticed Sonia's plate.

"Hey, Miss, don't you like the little green things?"

"Are they aubergine stones? Are we supposed to spit them?" Charlotte asked, alarmed.

"No, they're little flower buds called *capperi*, capers," Sonia said, trying to divert attention from her to the cause of her problem.

"Sir, Sir! Miss is leaving her food," Ryan shouted as if Brad was sitting at a table on the other end of the dining room rather than just opposite him.

Sonia quickly ran through her options in her mind. One, admit to it and wear the 'dunce' hat. Two, feign an allergy. Three, pretend that she'd set aside the best bits for last.

She immediately ruled out option two. It wasn't fair to people who really suffered from allergies. Option three was dangerous because she would have to eat the capers to prove it. Option one was the only one left. Sonia was about to open her mouth and admit her dislike of capers, when a chant rose from the table.

"Tinker, tailor, soldier, sailor, rich man…"

No, no, no! Charlotte, Laura and Hazel were going to assign her a husband based on her discarded capers. Sonia quickly counted ahead. Damn, it was going to land on sailor again! Extreme measures were urgently required. Sonia stabbed one of the capers with her fork and popped it into her mouth.

"Miss, you've cheated. It was going to be sailor!" Charlotte protested.

"What's wrong with sailors?" Laura asked.

"They cheat on you at every port," Hazel answered.

"Tinker is bad too. I wouldn't like a man who spends all his time tinkering with stuff," Laura said.

"You're so dumb! A tinker was a man who went around repairing metal pots," Charlotte said.

"Sailors are great. Mr. Wilson is a sailor," Aidan said.

Sonia wished that the ground could swallow her and spit her out on the other side of the planet, even if that was the middle of the Pacific Ocean, even if she had to hitch a lift from a sailor. Anyone but Brad.

"There are no tinkers anymore. This rhyme is stupid," Laura scoffed.

"We need a new one," Hazel said.

"Yes, one for boys. For Mr. Wilson!"

Oh no. All because of a caper. "They're serving the pudding," Sonia shrilled. Never had she been this excited about *panna cotta*.

But Charlotte was already counting the gnocchi on Brad's plate. "Teacher, tailor, soldier, sailor, rich woman, poor woman, homeless woman, thief…"

Just as Charlotte was about to shout "Teacher," Brad struck the last gnocchi with his knife and sliced it in two.

"Mr. Wilson, you've cheated too!"

"Gnocchi are for eating," he said, scooping a few into his spoon and eating them.

"Yes, let's finish our plates or we won't get any pudding anytime soon," Aidan said, and everyone returned to work on their plates except Ryan, who had already finished his.

But Sonia still had the caper stuck between her cheek and her gum. Before she could eat anything, she needed to swallow it with some water. The bottle of natural water was empty and the sparkly one was by Brad's side. She had no wish to ask him to pass it—or indeed speak to him about anything for any reason—so she leaned over to try to reach the bottle by herself. Doing so, her knuckles hit Brad's glass and toppled it. Sparkly water spilled and ran over the satiny tablecloth, sizzling and fizzling at the contact with the starched surface, spilling over the table's edge and straight into Brad's lap.

"I'm sorry!" Sonia grabbed the nearest napkin and instinctively made to dab Brad's groin but he grabbed her wrist and held it mid-air. He looked at her with his eyes wide open, shaking his head in disbelief. What the heck was she thinking of doing? And Sonia's cheeks flushed as hot as the sun.

"I'm really sorry." *About tipping your glass but mostly about the idiotic idea that I should mop up the water from your trousers.*

"It's okay," he said, letting out a breath that probably meant 'that was close'.

Not a moment too soon, the waiter arrived with the *panna cotta* and Brad asked him for some paper tissues. Sonia noticed that the waiter didn't try to dab Brad's trousers.

When the meal was finally over, Sonia ensured that all the girls were in their rooms and their lights were off, then she retreated to the safety of her suite.

As she opened the door and saw the half-drank limoncello bottle, the tulle bed curtains and the pretty little sofa, everything felt empty and pointless, like a doily without a cake. Something — or someone — was missing.

You should have thought about that before letting Brad slip into your heart.

She stepped into the shower and let the warm water pummel her skin and wash away the sand, the salt and any last traces of Brad's kiss. *A metaphorical catharsis.* If she could rub Brad off her skin with a brush and soap, she would have scoured herself raw. When she turned off the shower, she felt new, strong and clean — and ready to step into a life of men-free self-sufficiency.

But as she saw a crumpled dark green T-shirt abandoned on the floor by the sink, her heart twisted in her chest. *Brad's T-shirt.* She surveyed it then squatted, picked it up and, before she could stop herself, she lifted it to her nose. She closed her eyes. It smelled of

Brad. Her heart swirled with memories of his skin, and her entire body ached for him.

Until the image of her mother bending down to pick up her father's dirty laundry stung her. *You think that the sun shines out of his dirty laundry, but he's just like all the other men.* She balled up the T-shirt and stuffed it inside one of the hotel's laundry bags, then tied it with a tight knot. Judging by what the smell did to her brain, that T-shirt was a veritable biological hazard.

She was going to return the item to the offender and tell Mr.-Wonderful-Wilson where men should stick their dirty laundry if they couldn't be bothered to pick it up from the floor themselves.

She slipped into her nightdress, wrapped herself in the hotel's terry robe, and marched out of the room.

The door of room three-twenty opened almost immediately after she rapped on it. Brad's expression morphed from surprise to smile to grin, killer dimples included — and she forgot why she had come.

Chapter Ten

At suppertime Brad had noticed the tense lines on Sonia's face and had hoped that she wasn't upset. He'd also noticed that she was still wearing her bikini, judging by the strings knotted at the nape of her neck. Earlier, at the floating platform, it had taken every gentlemanly bone in his body to stop him from undoing that knot and traveling her neck with his lips. God, what had he been thinking?

He hoped that the tension on her face was due to tiredness or trouble from the kids. He did *not* want it to be about the kiss. He couldn't bear the thought of having upset her. That was why he was stepping back, recovering their distance before destroyed her life like he had destroyed Frances'.

He looked around his new room. It had a comfy-looking bed where he could sleep indoors, a bathroom where nobody would walk in on him and a small balcony where he would *not* spend the night. It looked out onto the same citrus orchard as the honeymoon suite, only two floors down, so the scent of the blossoms was stronger. There was absolutely nothing wrong with this room.

Still, something was missing. Brad sank on his haunches as he admitted to himself what was both missing and being missed. *Sonia.* Damn, he missed her.

A knock. He jumped up and went to the door. Anything to be distracted from his nostalgia.

And it was Sonia.

His heart kicked his ribs. Hard. She was wrapped in a white dressing gown that highlighted her tan and showed glimpses of a lacey nightdress. Her curls were gathered in a messy bun, rebellious strands breaking loose in places, exposing the perfect, delicious curve of her neck. Too much for a man to bear. "Hi." His voice came out rougher than expected.

"Hi." Her bellicose manner disappeared and her expression became uncertain, while her arms fell by her sides and a laundry bag hung limply from her hand.

She gave no hint that she might want to walk in, so he leaned against the door-jamb with forced nonchalance, as if he wasn't aching to scoop her off the ground and lay her on the bed to carry on from where they'd left off at the sea. "What can I do for you?" he asked, given that the reason for her visit wasn't forthcoming.

"I"—she bit her bottom lip—"was wondering if your room is okay?"

"Come and see it," he heard himself say, realizing that he'd been waiting just for that.

Danger. Keep her out.

No, it would be fine, so long as he didn't shut the door. Nothing that they would regret could happen with the door open. He stepped to the side to give her space to walk in without brushing against him and he kept holding on to the door for dear life.

As soon as she entered, room three-twenty suddenly looked as lovely as the honeymoon suite. Brad swallowed hard.

She looked around but her gaze seemed distracted, as if her mind was on some distant shores. *Mondello's shores.* He must apologize for that kiss.

"I'm sorry."

She looked at him. "About...?" She lifted the bag.

"About what happened at the beach."

"Ah-h. That." Her face sank, taking his heart down with it too.

He'd given the wrong answer. "And about the contents of that bag, whatever it is."

She shook her head almost imperceptibly and swept past him and out onto the balcony. Her shoulders lifted as she breathed in, then she swiveled around and pinned him with fire dancing in her eyes. "I'm not sorry about that kiss, Brad."

At that, his world spun. He had to press his feet hard against the floor tiles. *Keep away. You'll only hurt her. You've hurt her already.*

"But don't worry. That is not why I've come. I've come to return the dirty laundry you left on the floor." She dropped the bag on the desk.

"It's easier for everyone if we pretend that that kiss never happened," he said.

She clenched her fists. "Brad, a kiss like that could not be a mistake—or even chance. You can call it a moment of weakness, but never, *ever* call it a mistake. Unintentional? Yes. Unprofessional? Most. Unwise? For sure. But"—she shook her finger at him—"I will never allow that kiss to be tarnished by regret. I've already got enough of that sloshing about in my heart. I want to treasure the memory of that kiss because it won't happen again, with you or anyone else." Her whole body was visibly quivering, humming with energy. She took a breath, then. "And even if it did happen again, it wouldn't be the same with somebody else because, whether you like it or not, Brad Wilson, whether you meant it or not, in your arms I felt safe, protected and cherished. That kiss was happiness in technicolor, pleasure in four dimensions. Whatever you say or do now, that kiss will always hold a place of honor in my precious memories treasure chest."

She marched toward the door with her chin tilted up defiantly, exposing her lips like an offering. And that was more than a man could take.

She had come to his room to return his dirty laundry and to tell him off about it. Okay, *mostly* to tell him off about it. But she certainly hadn't meant to tell him what that kiss had meant to her or what she had felt when she was in his arms. All that stuff had burst out of her because of her anger, but now she was just as furious with herself as she had originally been with him.

As she stormed toward the door, her heart pounding with too many feelings to name, a hot hand grabbed her arm. She spun around and her gaze locked into Brad's. And that instantly unraveled her. His green eyes, deep and murky with desire like a lake agitated by a current, his musky sweet scent, the burning of his hand on her skin, all rocked her on her heels and tipped her onto her toes. Her eyes fluttered closed and her lips made soft, delicious contact with his. At that, all thoughts, reason and wisdom evaporated like puddles of spring rain under the Sicilian sun.

A soft click heralded the shutting of the door, which he had been holding like a life buoy, and he pulled her hungrily to him and deepened the kiss. Stars twinkled in the back of her eyes, melting her insides into a pot of liquid desire. He cradled the back of her skull and caressed her cheekbones with his thumb. Suddenly the moonlight was brighter, the duvet silkier, the fragrance of the citrus blossom headier. That scent reminded her of the night before, when they'd drunk limoncello on the terrace and opened their hearts to each other. Now they were about to open their bodies.

He broke the kiss and whispered into her mouth, "I don't want you to do anything that you will regret."

"I'm not the one who's been doing the regretting, Brad," she answered. She slipped the clip out of her hair that held her bun, releasing a cascade of defiant curls. "And if you make love the way you kiss, there won't be any regrets here."

As he let his tongue caress her lips while he cupped her breasts through the dressing gown, she let out a soft moan. With a throaty growl, he hitched her legs around his waist, carried her to the bed as if she weighed nothing and laid her down with a gentleness that was at odds with the rawness of the desire in his eyes.

He pulled his T-shirt from his back, the way men do, standing at the end of the bed with his pajama slacks hanging low on his narrow hips, exposing the dark hair rising up from the waistband.

With his gorgeous chest completely exposed, he sat on the edge of the bed. Sonia rolled onto her side, reaching for his slacks' waist but he stopped her. "Not yet. It's your turn now."

He rolled her onto her back and undid the knot of her dressing gown, unwrapping her like a delicate parcel. He slipped her nightie off from under her and discarded it over her head. He let a long, admiring gaze sweep over her body, then he closed his eyes and sighed. "I'm glad I hadn't known earlier how beautiful you are."

"Why?"

She pulled him down onto her, eager to feel his skin against hers. He smelled both familiar and new. She had smelled his delicious scent before, but now it was rawer and hotter.

He opened his eyes again, his pupils wide with desire. "Because I would have done inappropriate things, like this." He brushed his lips on her neck, giving her delicious goosebumps. His breath, soft and moist, brushed across her skin and down her collarbones as he kissed her, trailing his way to the swell of her breast. When he reached her nipple and circled it with his tongue, she couldn't help writhing with pleasure.

He descended into the valley between her breasts and climbed up to the other side, where he played havoc with her other nipple. She let out a deep moan and dug her fingers in his lush dark hair as pleasure spread all over her body, pooling between her legs, while his heart thumped through his chest against her tummy.

He smiled then traced her midline, playing circles around her navel with his tongue and stroking the inside of her thighs with his hands, gentling her legs apart.

When he reached between her legs, he looked up at her, as if asking for permission.

"I want you inside me," she breathed jaggedly.

"Not yet." He circled her wetness with his tongue and she gasped as her entire body throbbed with pleasure. He explored, teased, caressed, delicately but thoroughly, with his tongue. He played her like a beautiful musical instrument and she let out low, deep moans. He took her all the way to a shuddering climax, where time and space ceased to exist and her body was flooded with unbelievable pleasure.

As soon as she had regained control of her limbs, she slipped down his slacks. "Come inside me, Brad," she whispered.

"I haven't got a condom."

So he hadn't planned for this. And he wasn't someone who carried condoms in his wallet just in case opportunities arose, which was nice to know. But it was objectively inconvenient.

"Never mind. I'm at the end of my cycle. I can't get pregnant. And I don't have any STDs."

"If you'd rather—"

She silenced him with a kiss and interlaced her fingers with his. "I want you to come inside me, Brad."

He eased himself into her joyfully, easily. And as she felt his hard width inside her, she felt a connection like she had never had with anyone before. They fit into each other like two missing pieces. They fit like they belonged.

He thrust into her gently at first, then faster. She hooked her thighs around his waist, tilting her hips to let him in deeper, filling herself with him as if she would never have enough. She held him with her arms, her legs and with the muscles deep inside her. *Stay here forever, where you belong*.

He stopped and looked at her with hooded eyes. "I want you to come again," he said. Then he slid his hands under her buttocks, cupping them to angle her until he was pressing all the right places, both in and out.

"I don't thi—"

He silenced her with a kiss and continued to move like the waves of a calm sea, slowly, deeply and so deliciously that, moments later, Sonia dug her fingertips into his back and cried out his name as waves of pleasure took her over the edge again. At the same time, his body grew taut, he let out a deep groan and filled her with his seed. Then he kissed her neck again, panting, and rolled over.

"I hadn't realized sex could be like this," she said candidly.

He smiled then stared at the moon through the French window. "You must have come across some lousy lovers."

"I only had sex that once, when I was sixteen."

He turned to face her. "Thank you for trusting me, Sonia."

"Would it be too lame a joke if I answered, *my pleasure*?"

He ran a finger through one of her curls. "It wouldn't if you let me check that it's true." He kissed her neck and she wrapped her arms around him and they started all over again.

The last thing Sonia saw before falling asleep in Brad's arms was the dirty laundry bag, sitting on the desk, perfectly forgotten.

* * * *

When the halo of dawn penetrated the room through the open curtains, the first thing Brad saw was a cascade of licorice curls on his pillow. It took him a few seconds to register that they were not his. Sonia was asleep in his bed. It had really happened. That first hungry kiss that had shattered the ice… Their bodies intertwined… Her soft whimpers and moans as he kissed every inch of her skin and took her over the edge again and again… And the explosive feeling of being inside her… It had all happened.

A thought squeezed his belly. They hadn't used a condom. He hadn't packed any — why would he need them on a school trip? — but he would have stopped if she hadn't assured him that she was at the end of her cycle and asked him to carry on to the end. But what if her cycle was irregular and she did get pregnant? Strangely, the thought of having a child with Sonia didn't terrify him. What terrified him was the impact that it would have on her. How would she cope, after what she had already been through? Her situation now was nothing like when she had been sixteen and living in her parents' home. And, of course, he'd do the honorable thing and marry her, if she would have him. An unexpected lightheadedness took hold of him as he wished that things would follow precisely that course. It would be so easy and wonderful, no agonizing over pasts and futures. He couldn't imagine anything sweeter than making love to Sonia every night and waking up with her in his arms every morning.

'In your arms I felt safe, protected and cherished,' she had told him the previous night, making his heart swell with happiness. But she couldn't have possibly meant it. It had to have been one of those things said in moment of anger. He had epically failed to protect Frances and he must not be given the chance to destroy someone else's life all over again. He couldn't look after

anyone, let alone a baby and a woman who had already suffered enough. He didn't deserve to.

Her mouth puckered as she stirred in her sleep and turned onto her back. He followed the perfect curve of her forehead and nose, her delicious lips, that sweetest chin and her lovely neck all the way to a soft swelling peeking out from under the bedcovers. Desire stirred again inside him. *Don't even think about it.* She deserved a better man — someone whole and wholesome, not cracked and crushed by trauma and guilt, someone capable to protect her from harm.

That man wasn't him, so he had better get out of that bed double quick, start reeling their relationship back to what it should have been and stop imagining that his child was growing inside her. He had to put last night behind him and forget how good making love to Sonia had felt. Most of all, forget her.

He dragged himself out of bed, picked out the items that belonged to him from the clothes strewn on the floor and pulled them on. Before leaving the room, he grabbed the hotel's writing pad, scribbled *Sorry* and left it by her bedside.

At the noise of a door clicking shut, Sonia's eyes fluttered open. That sound triggered memories of the night before, when the closing of the door had Braded the beginning of her spiraling into a whirlpool of pleasure in Brad's arms. Where was he? He must have gone to the bathroom.

Their lovemaking had been as far from the clumsy and hurried affair she had had with Callum as a coughing fit was from a soprano's trill. Had it been simply the difference between the suavity and experience of a thirty-year-old and the unpolished rush of a sixteen-year-old or was there more? Something to do with…the heart? *God help me. I can't be falling in love with Brad.*

She couldn't tell, but what she *could* tell was that even just standing close to Brad sent her heart cavorting in her chest. Feeling his fingers on her skin made her sizzle with electricity. And kissing him — a frisson went up her back at the mere thought — made fireworks explode inside her skull.

Last night, there had been more than fingers on skin and kisses. Their entire bodies had fused into one. It had been breathtaking, toe-curling, tummy-fluttering.

But they had used no protection. Her belly clenched. She was at the tail end of her cycle, but that wasn't the most reliable method of contraception around.

Stupid idiot. I should have known better.

Anyway, she was most likely infertile after the abortion and the complications, so the chances of getting pregnant were very low indeed. A sigh escaped her throat. *I want Brad's baby.*

Outlandish. Ridiculous. Why ever would she want Brad's baby? Imagine the scandal at school. Being a single mum now would be much easier than it would have been when she was sixteen, but still… Besides, it wouldn't be right to get together just for the sake of the baby. Brad was still besotted with his dead girlfriend, plus he had clearly told her that he was sorry about the kiss at the beach. Their night of passion had been just that — one night of runaway, reckless passion.

But why would he carry on making love to her if, as a doctor, he must have known full well how unreliable a contraceptive method they were using? And knowing that she had got pregnant by accident before. Maybe he didn't mind the chance.

Stop dreaming.

As soon as one man showed her some interest, she'd immediately started building sandcastles around it. What had happened the previous night had been a moment of weakness born of the hot scirocco and the heady *zagara*. Brad wasn't hers to keep, to cling on to, to snuggle up in bed with on the morning after. In fact, he wasn't there. By her side, there were only crinkled bedsheets.

He must be in the bathroom. *He would have come back by now.* He must have rushed to wake up the kids. *Not at a quarter past six.*

A pang of sadness clamped around her heart. It was the same feeling of abandonment she had felt when Callum had turned his back on her and their baby. Now she must get up, dust herself off and behave as professionally as she could. She had work to do and the kids must not know what an awful example she was setting. She sat up and saw the hotel's notepad resting on her bedside table with something scribbled on it.

Sorry. It was Brad's handwriting.

A vise clamped around her heart. *No, it's not about the dirty laundry he left on the floor.* It was the confirmation of what she had just worked out — that Brad wasn't for her. What had happened between them that night had been another moment of weakness, not the beginning of something. She had already figured it out, so why were tears welling in her eyes?

She got up and washed her face in the bathroom. Then she got dressed, sneaked out into the corridor and back up to her suite. The children mustn't know anything about it.

Only, the children already knew. When Sonia did her wake-up call around, Charlotte popped her head around her door. "Miss Alletti, I was looking for you last night. I knocked on your door but you didn't open it." Her eyes were brimming with reproach.

Sonia's blood rippled in her veins. "I must have been fast asleep. Why? What was the matter?"

"I needed painkillers for a migraine."

"You should have asked Mr. Wilson. He carries the medicines," Laura suggested groggily from her bed.

"That wouldn't have changed anything. They're in the same room," Charlotte retorted, turning back to Laura.

Laura must have told Charlotte that she had found her and Brad in the same room. How many other people had she told? Goosebumps sprang up on Sonia's arms.

"Oh yeah, of course." Laura turned around and pulled the covers over her head.

"Has your migraine gone now?" Sonia felt like Charlotte's migraine might be migrating on to her.

"Yes, thank you, Miss."

"Good. Now get ready and I'll see you downstairs for breakfast at seven-thirty."

Sonia pulled the door closed with intention, as if by doing that she could trap any gossip about her and Brad in that room. What a cruel piece of luck, that the night when they hadn't done anything should be the one that would give them away. Like a guardian angel, Laura had saved them. Pity she hadn't knocked on their door last night too.

Chapter Eleven

When he saw Sonia plonk her bag onto the seat next to his, Brad took the message and looked for somewhere else to sit. She had avoided him at breakfast, limiting their exchanges to the bare minimum necessary, and Brad couldn't blame her or say that he was surprised. It certainly made regaining his distance much easier. But it still hurt.

Aidan was all by himself, which was unusual, so Brad decided to sit with him and check that he was all right.

"How's stuff with you, big boy?"

"I'm not sure, Sir."

"What's the matter?"

"Girls."

Tell me about it. "What about them?"

"One moment they like you, the next they hate you."

"Ah. That's not just girls. Boys do that too. Do you think that you might have done something that upset her?"

"I don't think so. If I ask her, she'll say no. Girls say no even when it's not true and you're supposed to ask a million more times or somehow 'get' it out of her yourself, but you never can."

"Well, at least you've worked that out."

"Why are girls so complicated?"

"People are not just what we see. There's a lot behind them—things that have happened in their past, people they've known—that we have no idea about. And all that stuff makes them behave in ways that sometimes makes no sense to you unless you know all that's happened to them before. It's not just girls. Everyone does that."

Aidan groaned. "And what am I supposed to do about it?"

Oh God, I'm the last person who should give the boy advice! "Do you really care about that girl?"

"Yes."

"Then…be forgiving. Be patient. Be there for her." Brad sighed quietly. "Now, show me what games you've got on your phone."

It didn't take them long to reach their twinned school, the Liceo Classico Pirandello. It sat on a set of steps like a Greek temple and was decorated with an imposing collection of columns in the mock-Roman fascist style. In stark contrast with the belligerence of the building, their liaison, a dark-haired teacher called Valeria, welcomed them warmly.

"Have you had a nice trip so far?" she asked them.

"Very much," Jake said.

"Absolutely," Katie replied.

Brad didn't reply and noticed that Sonia didn't either.

Valeria addressed the children in her language and they replied in fluent Italian.

"Wow, I wasn't expecting your Italian to be so good. I'm now wondering if you'll find some of the work that I've prepared for you a little too easy."

The children's language competence was a credit to Sonia's hard work, Brad thought. She was such a good teacher. *And a wonderful woman in many, many ways.*

"Don't worry, *Professoressa*. We're very good at easy work!" Ryan called out, and everyone laughed.

"I'm sure you are." Valeria smiled. "Follow me."

She led them into the building, which consisted of two floors of classrooms surrounding a large central courtyard a bit like the kind one might find in a Roman villa. There was no grass anywhere and only a handful of scraggy trees emerging from square holes in the ubiquitous cement.

"The students are having their first lesson after their mid-morning break," Valeria explained. "They're taught in tutor groups for all subjects and remain in their classrooms while the teachers move from one classroom to another at the sound of the bell. You'll be with this class." She knocked on a door and opened it. The metal legs of thirty chairs scraped the tiled floor as thirty students stood up to welcome the visitors. The formality of the gesture felt at odds with the students' lack of uniforms.

In front of the blackboard stood a tall, dark young man. He looked way too suave and debonair to belong to that classroom, where the paint peeled off the ceiling and the venetian blinds hung askew. Unbelievably, not a speck of chalk had fallen off his hand and landed on his dark blue jacket. His hair was slightly long at the top and fashionably disheveled, and his beige and blue loafers echoed back to his beige jeans and the blue jacket. It was obvious that he hadn't just tossed on the first garments he had found in his cupboard.

"*Benvenuti*, welcome, to all our visitors from England. *Ave*! I'm *Professore* Liotta." The Latin greeting and the Latin writing on the board suggested that he must be the kids' Latin teacher.

There was more scraping of chairs as everyone was offered a seat, until the chairs ran out and Brad and Sonia were left without. At that, *Professore* Liotta whipped out his chair from behind his desk and offered it to Sonia with a flourish. There was nothing wrong with that gesture, and Brad wouldn't have expected to be offered a seat if there was still a lady standing. But the way the other man's gaze lingered on Sonia a beat too long made his skin crawl. *I have no claim over her. I can't be jealous.*

He leaned against the wall and watched *Professore* Liotta continue the lesson. On the board, in perfect calligraphy, was Catullus' poem number LXXV.

Odi et amo. Quare id faciam fortasse requiris.
Nescio, sed fieri sentio et excrucior.

I hate and I love. Why would I do that, perhaps you'll ask.
I don't know, but I can feel it happening and I'm tortured.

The elegiac couplet resonated with Brad. He too was tortured. He needed — and wanted — to keep away from Sonia, and yet he couldn't bear the distance they were placing between them.

As the man recited the poem, darting glances at Sonia, his inflection as melodious as a mandolin, Brad's jealousy mounted. *He's not flirting. He's just Italian.*

But so was Sonia. Maybe *Professore* Liotta could relate to her in ways that would speak straight to her Italian heart. *Then I should be happy for her. I have no claim over her. Let her find happiness with those who can give it to her.* Brad clenched his fists in his pockets and tried not to frown.

When he had finished talking about the poem, *Professore* Liotta asked his students to introduce themselves, then he asked the visiting students and Jake and Katie. When he moved on to Sonia, she turned to face the kids and said, "I'm Sonia Alletti, I teach Italian at Oakton School and I'm very glad to be here. Thank you for welcoming us."

The man had only just finished folding his arms and resting his chin on his hand in a pose of interested concentration when she finished speaking, surprising Brad. "Well, it's *really* nice to have you with us, *Professoressa* Alletti," he drawled. Then the man introduced himself, including details about his personal life, his marital status and his semi-pro windsurfing status. He was about to move on to the next part of the lesson when Sonia interrupted him.

"And we've also got our head of biology, *Professore* Brad Wilson"—she flipped a hand in Brad's direction, though avoiding eye contact—"who's not just a scientist but also an amazing linguist and has learned all the Italian he knows—which is quite a lot—in the hours we've spent on the coach."

He was surely glad to have learned enough to be able to follow what she was saying about him. *Why should I care what she thinks of me?*

"But *Professore* Wilson is not just very gifted. He's also very kind," she continued, "because he stepped in at the last minute to accompany our trip. Without him, we wouldn't be with you today."

Very kind? Didn't she hate him for running off after what there had been between them? For leaving a one-word note because he was too cowardly and afraid of his weakness to talk things through like an adult? Not only did her words sound sincere, but she had interrupted *Professore* Liotta to make sure his introduction wasn't skipped, and that was an objective fact. With his heart feeling like a helium balloon, Brad flashed the class a grin.

"If, without him, you wouldn't have been here, then we must thank Mr. Wilson very much," *Professore* Liotta said, using the singular 'you', *tu*, that singled her out of the group and addressed her informally, as if they had known each other before, then he went on with the lesson.

Sonia feared that she might have exposed herself in her spontaneous and enthusiastic praise of Brad. She didn't care if *Professore* Liotta imagined her having a crush on Brad. In fact, she would have loved him to think that she was immune to his flirting, after the unbelievable rudeness with which he had blanked Brad as if he wasn't in the room. But she didn't want to offer more fuel for her students to gossip about. It hadn't been wise to talk so generously about him. She could have asked him to introduce himself, but the other man's patent antipathy toward him had made her angry. It wasn't about Brad. *Oh yeah?* No, it was a matter of principle, and she would have reacted the same way if the man had been rude to anyone. *Really?*

The next lesson was philosophy. A teacher who looked old enough to have been pals with Aristotle shuffled into the room.

"Don't let appearances fool you. He's a force to be reckoned with," Valeria whispered in her ear. "The kids will be fine with him. Come on. Let me show you those assessment records we've talked about."

Sonia told Jake and Katie, who were sitting next to her, that she'd be going to the staffroom with Valeria. Then she gestured to Brad, who was leaning against the wall at the opposite end of the room. He must have misunderstood her signal because, instead of staying in the classroom, he joined Sonia and Valeria in the corridor. It was too late to correct the misunderstanding.

"I asked Valeria to show me how they record assessment data," she informed him.

A large oval table sat in the middle of the semi-dark staffroom. Some seats had been claimed with jackets and cardigans that were too warm to be worn in April, and Sonia concluded that they must have been sacrificed as permanent placeholders. Brad lingered to study a school photo that hung on one of the walls, while Valeria led Sonia to a group of teachers in one corner, who seemed a lot friendlier than the two scowling at the oval table.

"Your Italian is wonderful. And I heard that your students did really well in Antonio's Latin lesson," a pretty young female teacher told her.

"Thank you. There's nothing a teacher likes to hear more."

"Ah! You must be the Italian teacher from England! Antonio just told me about you. He told me that you were lovely but I couldn't imagine how petite and cute you were! A doll," a matronly woman piped loudly as she tottered over to them. "I'm Maria Grassi, the headteacher."

Sonia had forgotten about Italian effusiveness and felt heat rise up her cheeks. She was pulled into the warmest full-bosom embrace while, out of the corner of her eye, she saw Brad walk over, followed by a thunderous cloud. Had he heard about the Latin teacher's comment? Was he jealous? *I'm fantasizing.*

As soon as she spotted Brad, the pretty young teacher's face lit up in the same way the hotel receptionist's had — and the way most women's seemed to.

"Are you together?" the head teacher asked, sounding hopeful.

"No," Sonia said.

"Yes," Brad said at the same time.

Sonia felt her cheeks on fire. Of course the headteacher hadn't meant 'together', as in being a couple. *Stop thinking of Brad as anything but a colleague.*

"I mean, yes, we are. This is my colleague, Brad Wilson, the head of biology."

"Antonio didn't tell me about you," the headteacher said candidly.

The thunder in Brad's eyes turned to lightning.

"You are *proprio bel* — ahem, *benvenuto*." The headteacher deftly recovered her slip from 'most handsome' to 'most welcome', then returned them to Valeria and tottered off.

Valeria showed Sonia and Brad the school's pupil assessment records until the bell rang, loud and shrill. "I think that perhaps we should rescue your kids from a second hour of philosophy in a foreign language. If I remember well, there's a boy who prefers easy work."

"Ah, that would be Ryan. And, yes, I think that you're right," Sonia said.

So they left the staffroom and went out into the courtyard, which had been turned into a volleyball court for a PE lesson. As they were walking around the court, careful to steer clear of the game, *Professore* Liotta emerged from another door. As soon as he saw them, his supercilious frown stretched into a smarmy smile that was unabashedly directed at Sonia. Instead of skirting the wall, as they were doing, he cut across one corner of the court.

It all happened in fractions of a second. One moment the ball was hurtling toward *Professore* Liotta's head, the next it was being deflected by Brad with a giant leap.

"*Ma che cazzo?*" *Professore* Liotta shouted at Brad, who had temporarily invaded his personal space, even if he'd not actually brushed him. Then the man quickly glanced at Sonia, probably to check if she had noticed his less-than-polite language.

"*Grazie!*" the volleyball players shouted at Brad.

"That ball was going for your head," Brad told the man, rubbing the knuckles that had taken the brunt of the impact.

Professore Liotta didn't thank him but mumbled something under his breath, adjusted his tie and walked on. Sonia couldn't help comparing the two men—a comparison from which Brad emerged a million times the winner.

The end-of-school bell rang at one-thirty and they went for lunch in a hearty *trattoria* halfway to their next destination. Then, with their stomachs full of pasta, everyone but Sonia slept through the next stretch of their journey to Caltagirone, the home of Sicilian ceramics.

As soon as she saw the ceramic workshop perched on a little hill on the outskirts of the town of Caltagirone, she thought of Jack and Jill, tumbling down the hill with their pails of water. Only Jack and Jill were Brad and her, and the pails of water were terracotta jugs. *You and Brad, falling in love, breaking your lives to pieces.* She shook her head as if to shake the thought out.

A young woman with dark, straight hair and a generous chest stood on the threshold of the low concrete building. She was holding a plump baby around six months old with lively eyes and a ready smile. A pink hairband with a pink rosette was wrapped around the baby's hairless head, more as a sex identifier than a hairstyling item.

"Welcome to our ceramic studio," she said with a warm smile, as soon as they had gathered around her. But the factory wasn't the main attraction there.

Ryan was the first to offer his finger to the baby, who immediately wrapped her chubby little hand around it. "She likes me! She likes me!" he shouted.

"What's her name?"

"How is she?"

"Has she got any teeth?"

The other kids' questions came in thick and fast.

"She's named Rosa and she's seven months old. Yes, she has two teeth and I don't advise you to try them. Well, well, if your Italian isn't a hundred times better than I expected," the woman said. "That's great. I won't have to use my terrible English on you. My name is Giovanna. Come… Follow me."

They followed Giovanna — or, actually, the baby — into a room that was an explosion of color and breakable items.

"Take your backpacks off your backs," Sonia called. "Don't move abruptly and don't push."

"This is the finished product," Giovanna said, pointing to the shelves full of dishes, bowls and vases decorated in the most cheerful yellows, blues and greens. "They're all handmade and hand-painted."

"By the baby?" Ryan asked.

"Not yet. For now, just my mum and dad, my sister and me."

"What are these for?" Ryan asked again, pointing to a pair of life-sized ceramic heads.

"Ah, these. They are flowerpots but their story is a little gruesome. I'm not sure if I should tell you. What does your teacher say?" Giovanna turned to Sonia.

"It's fine, but I won't translate." She was sure that the children would stretch their Italian to the limit for the sake of a gruesome story.

"The legend of the *Testa di Moro,* Moor's head, says that when the Arabs ruled Sicily, around the year 1000, a beautiful girl lived in Palermo. She was always tending her plants at the balcony and, one day, a handsome Moor — an Arab — saw her and fell head-over-heels in love with her. He rushed up to her flat and declared his love with such passion that the girl reciprocated. Unfortunately, though, the girl soon found out that her beloved was due to return to Arabia, where he had a wife and children. Feeling desperate and betrayed, she waited for him to fall asleep then…cut off his head."

"Ouch!" Ryan said.

"She kept his head, so that he would never leave her, and turned it into a vase —"

"Yuk!"

"Where she grew basil and watered it with her tears. Basil is the symbol of kings, and that's why our ceramic heads have a crown. The basil grew very well and all the girl's neighbors made vases in the shape of a Moor's head for their basil plants too."

Silence fell in the room. Sonia felt very sorry for the girl of the legend, perhaps even more on that day than she would have on another, but she could never imagine cutting Brad's head off or doing him any harm, even if he had sworn eternal love to her, which he definitely hadn't, while having a wife in another country, which she trusted he didn't. Then Rosa gurgled and everyone smiled again.

"Right… Let's go next door, where you can have a go at the potter's wheel," Giovanna said.

The pottery studio smelled of earth and was gray from top to bottom. Gray clay, gray shelves, gray pots, gray dust. It seemed short of a miracle that the wonderfully colorful artifacts next door could have come out of so much gray.

"Here is where we store the clay, over there is where we recycle it and over there are the wheels, where we shape the clay. We call it 'throwing'. We let the vases and plates dry on these shelves before we paint and glaze them next door then bake them in the kiln," Giovanna said, moving toward a machine that looked like a rotating table. "This one is a kick wheel, which you power with your foot. My dad loves it, while I prefer the electric one. It's a little harder to control the speed in the electric one, but it's not quite so much hard work as the kick wheel. Who wants to have a go at the wheel?"

Nobody volunteered, not even Ryan, perhaps because Giovanna had mentioned hard work. And the clay sat on the wheel looking sad and lonely.

"Perhaps a strong man like your teacher will have a go," Giovanna said, smiling at Brad.

"Go, Mr. Wilson. Go!" the boys shouted.

"Sure." Brad stepped out and sat down at the wheel.

"Now Mr. Wilson will 'throw' the clay —"

"Whoa! Watch out for flying clay," Ryan said.

"Which means shaping the clay at the wheel. He will make a vase like this. Now, Mr. Wilson, push the pedal up and down while you squeeze the clay between your hands, with good, equal pressure on both sides."

The clay yielded under Brad's hands. *Like I did last night.* They were the same hands that had wrapped her waist, followed the contour of her spine, brushed her cheeks ever so gently… Images of the night that had just passed flashed before her. Under those long, slender fingers of his, she had been like that clay. And the scary thing was that she wished to be there again.

"A little harder… Press with your thumb…" Giovanna hesitated then she turned to Sonia. "Would you mind holding Rosa?"

Sonia wasn't expecting it, and, before she had replied or knew what was happening, the baby was in her arms, gurgling and smiling. Instant pleasure flooded Sonia. She hadn't imagined that holding a baby could be so lovely. Rosa was so soft, she smelled so sweet and she was totally abandoned, totally trusting Sonia not to drop or harm her. Rosa put a chubby little hand on Sonia's cheek, which Sonia inflated, making Rosa giggle. Then the baby reached at Sonia's earring and frowned in extreme concentration. She was so sweet, so funny, so…lovely. *I could have had a baby all of my own.* Sonia chased the thought away and turned her attention to the pottery lesson.

She saw Giovanna putting her hands on top of Brad's. "Less gentle… Go harder on it. That's better."

The sight of a woman's hands on Brad's stabbed Sonia with spikes of raw, green venom. *I can't be jealous of someone who isn't mine.* But she was. Her jaw clenched, her arms tensed and her throat tightened. The baby whimpered.

"*No, piccola, non piangere,*" Sonia cooed. But babies couldn't be fooled. Rosa's lip quivered. Sonia felt just like that. Her face wrinkled then scrunched up. Sonia felt like that too. Then her little puckered mouth let out a wail. Oh, how Sonia wished she could wail too!

Giovanna whipped her head around. "Oh dear, she must be hungry. Sometimes she can smell the smell of another mum. Have you got a baby too?" she asked Sonia.

"Oh. No! No."

"Can you bear to hold her for a little more, so we can finish this pot?"

Sonia nodded, even though the 'we' Giovanna had used about Brad and her really irked Sonia. *Let go. He's not yours.*

Sonia turned Rosa around so that she could see her mum, and the baby shook her arms and legs with excitement. *There we go. A baby knows her mum.*

"This vase looks like Miss Alletti," Charlotte said, once the wheel was stopped and the vase was declared finished.

Sonia had to admit that there was a little similarity between her waist-to-hip ratio and the vase, even though she wasn't sure whether that was a good thing. Brad's cheeks went a red shade of purple and he shot up from the potter's seat.

Giovanna thanked Sonia for holding Rosa and said, "Right... Now it's time for our painting workshop," and led them into the room next door.

The painting studio was a world suspended between gray and color. It was scattered with artifacts at all stages of maturity, from fully painted and waiting to be glazed, to totally gray, with all the stages in between. Twenty-eight totally blank plates were laid out neatly on a long worktop, each next to a set of brushes and a color palette.

"Are we going to paint them?" Laura asked.

"Yes."

"And take them home?"

"Sure. I'll glaze them and bake them in the kiln, then I'll post them to your hotel, as I've agreed with your teacher."

"Yessss!"

A moment of happy chaos followed, until everyone had got a workstation and a plate to decorate.

"This is my sister, Angelina. She's the one who runs this room, together with our mum. I tend to do more wheel work. Feel free to ask her for help — or ask me. And here are some examples of patterns you can take inspiration from, but feel free to paint whatever makes you happy." The baby shook her arms in excitement at the word 'happy'.

"Miss Giovanna, can you help me?" Aidan called.

Giovanna turned to Sonia again. "As you've been so good with Rosa next door, would you mind holding her again?"

"My pleasure," Sonia said, welcoming the baby like an old friend while Giovanna went to help Aidan.

Rosa leaned heavily to Sonia's right in the way small children do when they want to be taken somewhere but can't yet communicate it with words. "Let's see what's over there," Sonia said in a voice that she had never used with anyone before—talking-to-a-baby voice—and followed Rosa's tilting angle.

Behind a floor-to-ceiling shelving unit, an old lady sat at a small table, painting. Rosa squealed, the old lady lifted her face and her deep wrinkles rearranged into a toothless smile.

"Granddaughter of mine!" she exclaimed in the local dialect. The woman's words were obviously meant for the baby but Sonia's heart filled with nostalgia for her grandmas, who had also spoken dialect when they had still been alive.

"Hello, Granny," Sonia greeted her in dialect and the old lady's smile-wrinkles deepened.

"I can't speak English and my Italian is bad, so I decided to hide here. But you speak dialect too?"

"I can. Not the others."

"Then I can talk to you. Take a seat. My name is Rosa. *Nonna* Rosa."

"I'm Sonia."

She sat on the wooden chair that *Nonna* offered her and adjusted Rosa on her lap. Rosa bounced up and down with excitement when her *nonna* gave her a clean brush and she started copying *Nonna's* paint strokes on Sonia's hand.

"Then I guess that baby Rosa must be named after you," Sonia said.

"Of course," the old woman said, straightening her hunched back a little. She was still painting the most delicate yellow flower on a blue-and-gray plate, even though she wasn't always looking at the plate. "Have you got children too?" the old lady asked.

"No, unfortunately."

"But you will,"Nonna Rosa stated, matter-of-factly.

"I don't think so."

"Why ever not?" She glanced at Sonia while she dipped her brush in the color without looking.

"I haven't got a man."

"But you will."

"I probably can't get pregnant."

"But these days doctors can do anything. Why do you think that you can't get pregnant?"

"I had a bad infection after...an operation when I was sixteen." Just then Sonia felt Brad's presence, the way she just did whenever he was near her. Inexplicably. Weirdly. Eerily, perhaps. But she turned around and, sure enough, he was right behind her.

"Here is the man for you," *Nonna* Rosa said, fixing her gaze on Brad intently. As he wasn't saying anything, she asked, "Does he understand me?"

"No."

"Then tell him what I said."

Sonia smiled nervously. It must be a joke.

"Tell him."

Sonia hesitated. Rosa's brush had now reached her neck but Sonia didn't feel ticklish. She just felt...worried.

"What's the matter? Is he engaged to someone else?"

"No, *Nonna*."

"Don't you like him?"

Sonia could feel the heat rising up her neck and pouring into her cheeks.

"He's handsome, isn't he?" *Nonna* pressed.

"Yes, he is."

"Well, tell him then that I said that he's the man for you. Go on. Tell him."

Sonia swallowed. "Brad, *Nonna* Rosa would like you to know that she thinks that you are very handsome." It was only a small lie and *Nonna* Rosa would never know.

"Thank you," Brad said.

Just then, Giovanna appeared around the shelving. "I've got plates to decorate for the grown-ups too. Come on over."

Sonia was only too pleased to leave that awkward conversation.

"Leave my granddaughter here to help me," *Nonna* Rosa said, and Sonia put the baby on her lap.

"It was nice meeting you, *Nonna* Rosa," she said to the old lady.

"My pleasure. And remember what I said."

"What did my mum tell you?" Giovanna asked Sonia when they were leaving.

"I think she likes playing matchmaker," Sonia said lightly.

"Don't underestimate her. She has a gift for these things. She saw my husband and my brother-in-law in the street and said that they would become her sons-in-law — before they'd ever even met my sister and me."

As they walked past the kids, there was rustling and hushing. Were they up to something naughty?

"Don't worry. They're fine," Giovanna said, steering her away as Sonia was trying to hang back. "Here is your workstation," she said, showing Sonia and Brad to a table tucked away behind a shelving unit. Jake and Katie were already busy painting their plates.

"Thank you. You really didn't need to do this. And I feel that we should be there with the kids, helping you out."

Giovanna shook her head. "There is absolutely no need. Your students are as good as gold. My sister and I can manage."

Sonia sat on one side of the table for four and Brad on the other.

"I'm crap at this," Jake said. "I hate art."

"Shut up and work," Katie said. Her plate was coming along really nicely, with patterns of flowers and birds.

What should she paint? *'Paint whatever makes you happy,'* Giovanna had told the kids. What made her happy? Sunlight scattered by the surface of the sea, rays of light filtering down the water column and reaching the underwater meadows, blades of seagrass swaying in the current. Yes, those things filled her with quiet happiness. Sonia dipped her brush into the blue first, then the green for the blades of the seagrass, white and red for the flowers. Then a splash of red for a starfish and the shadow of a fish. But as Sonia continued painting, almost in a trance, she suddenly noticed that the shadow of a fish swimming down from the surface had legs and wide shoulders — and a mop of coppery brown hair. Sonia quickly rinsed her brush and turned the legs into a fin and the hair into a tangled piece of seaweed so that it wasn't a man anymore. It wasn't Brad.

"I can't believe this, Brad." Jake put down his paintbrush. "You play football quite decently, swim like a dolphin and soak up languages like a computer. And you can even paint."

Brad's plate had a beautiful scene of what looked like a sunrise or sunset in a lemon grove. It was very much like the view from the balcony of their suite.

"Is there anything you can't do, man?" Jake asked rhetorically.

"Plenty," Brad said.

"I don't believe you. You're humble too. That's the truth. And it almost makes me sick how perfect you are."

"You're just sore because we beat you at table football after breakfast."

"Ah, I forgot table football, thanks. Doesn't he make you sick, Sonia?"

"Me?" Sonia felt like a student when the teacher asked them a question they weren't expecting.

"Sorry, darling, but I doubt you'll find that Brad makes women feel sick. Other things, surely, but not *sick*."

Jake lifted an eyebrow and peered into Sonia's face, as if to check whether his wife's statement was correct. Sonia felt her cheeks, still hot from *Nonna* Rosa's grilling, starting to heat up again. Did Katie know what had happened between her and Brad? Could she tell from the glow on Sonia's face, the way a woman can? Or was it tattooed on her forehead for all to read, and that was why *Nonna* Rosa had instantly paired them?

"I'm going to ask Giovanna for some more blue," she said, standing up.

"Yes, yes, you do that," Jake teased.

Sonia had to stop herself from actually running away from the table. She found the bottle of paint by the sink and decided to help herself to the blue without asking Giovanna. She desperately wanted to be alone, even if for the few seconds she could pretend to be choosing the right bottle. Maybe if she pretended to struggle unscrewing the lid, she could snatch a few more seconds. She was just doing that when she heard Brad's voice behind her.

"Can I open it for you?"

"Oh…er…yes, please." She handed him the bottle and he looked surprised when the lid almost flew off his hands because it was so loose.

He returned the bottle to her and shifted on his feet, as if he was about to say something but he wasn't really sure whether he should.

"Sonia, I just thought that I should let you know that last week they've announced a breakthrough treatment for women who have been made infertile by womb infections."

Sonia's jaw slackened. "Brad!"

"If you don't want to talk about it, that's fine. I totally understand."

"Did you hear me talk about it to *Nonna* Rosa? Did you actually understand us?"

"Some things, yes, I think, like the part when she asked you if I understood her and you said no."

"God, Brad, you should have told us! What did you understand?"

"That after you had the abortion—"

"Stop! Actually, I don't want to know." Had he also understood that the old lady had insisted she tell him that he was the right man for her? And that Sonia had fobbed her off by telling him something different?

Brad went on. "Sorry. I knew I shouldn't have said it. You might not even want children—and there would be nothing wrong with that. Absolutely nothing wrong. I just didn't want you to live in fear that you might not have children if you want them."

Brad was still shifting on his feet and avoiding her gaze like an eleven-year-old boy who was talking to a girl for the first time. Saying these things was clearly costing him. Why would he do it?

"Don't worry. I'm not fretting about children. If anything, I should concern myself with finding a man first."

"You will, Sonia. You are everything a woman needs to be. You've got everything going for you. A man who really loves you and appreciates you won't give a damn whether you can have children or not. He won't give a flipping toss about it!"

Sonia was struck by the energy with which he'd said that last sentence. It was very sweet, actually. "Thank you, Brad." She didn't say *I don't want a man in my life* because that wasn't true anymore. But the new truth was too sad. The only man she wanted wasn't available, at least not to her. "Thank you, Brad. And, by the way, you paint very well."

Chapter Twelve

It had been a strange day and Brad should have been glad to have a room of his own to retreat to. When was the last time he had been completely alone, with nobody to demand his attention? The previous night he should have been alone, but then things had gone the way they'd gone.

Don't think about it.

When he had been a surgeon, he'd always ensured that he had a space to retreat to when he needed to be on his own for a little while. When he'd switched to teaching and the students needed him just as much as his patients had, he'd found that he also needed his regular fix of solitude. That was why he had never agreed to move in with a woman, even with Frances. He had valued his own headspace too much. But now that he was about to get the luxury of ten hours' uninterrupted solitude, he missed Sonia. She infiltrated his every thought and she'd likely turn up in his dreams too. It had happened before.

He stripped out of his clothes and stepped into the shower. That should soothe him. But as soon as he found her hair clip resting on the soap holder, he was flooded with longing. It wasn't just his body that missed the incredible sex they'd had. His heart missed her too.

All through that day he had tried to think of her just as a colleague, but that hadn't stopped him feeling rejected when she had settled her bag on the coach seat next to hers, feeling jealous when the Italian teacher was flirting with her or crackling with happiness when she had introduced him to the class with the kindest words.

He dried himself and took a lemonade out of the minibar then pushed a chair out onto the balcony, turned off the lights in the room and sat outside. It struck him that the lemonade was standing in for the limoncello and the chair out on the balcony was in place of the bench where he'd sat with Sonia, like in a pathetic re-enactment of that night on the balcony together. He took a swig and sighed.

As his eyes got used to the darkness, the stars emerged from the night sky like diamond studs on deep blue velvet. He could distinguish Ursa Major, Ursa Minor and Orion. If only his eyes could accommodate to the darkness of his heart and tell him what was going on in there too.

* * * *

When Sonia could finally retreat to the suite *alone,* it felt like a relief. She bolted the door with the chain and latch, more as a precaution to keep herself inside than to stop intruders coming in.

The unfortunate but understandable absence of a TV in the honeymoon suite meant that Sonia had to resort to playing silly games on her phone to distract herself from memories of Brad sleeping out on the balcony — his long lashes on his sharp cheekbones — or coming out of the shower beaded with water, massaging her back with tortured eyes. She was sitting on a chair — never on the sofa where Brad had slept — playing yet another idiotic game when the phone rang in her hands, giving her a mighty shock. It was Mrs. Ashcroft's number.

"Hello, Sonia, how is the trip going?" Mrs. Ashcroft's voice sounded unnaturally cheery, which immediately put Sonia on the defensive.

"Very well. The children seem to be learning a lot and having a great time."

"And are you and Brad having a great time too?" There was some innuendo in the headteacher's tone.

Sonia tensed up. "Yes, I believe that Brad is very impressed with Sicily."

"Are you sure that he's impressed with Sicily and not with *you*?"

"Please, Mrs. Ashcroft, do tell me clearly what this call is about."

"Very well then, Sonia. I've received complaints that you and Brad are too busy with each other to look after the children in your ward. I would have expected this from Jake and Katie, of course, but not from *you two*."

The headteacher's last two words dripped with a contempt that stung Sonia like a barb dipped in acid.

Even Mrs. Ashcroft thinks that I'm unsuitable for Brad.

"And I've received reports that you're sharing a room."

"For two nights we had to share a room because the hotel was full and I had forgotten to amend the booking after Kate's accident. It was definitely not our choice, and we were both willing to pay for the extra room out of our pockets. Regarding the first point, could you give me some concrete examples?"

"I cannot expose the parents or the children who have raised their concern. But I can say that a child went looking for you in the night, in need of medicine, and you didn't answer your door. Had it been a more serious emergency, I cannot imagine what would have happened if you and Brad had been unreachable."

Charlotte. She must have told her mum and her mum must have complained to Mrs. Ashcroft. Hot shame pricked her eyes. She had promised the woman that she'd keep a special eye on Charlotte, but she had let both down. Sonia sank in the chair and bent double as if she could somehow curl herself into non-existence. This must be the lowest point in her career. One of the lowest in her life. "I am deeply sorry, Mrs. Ashcroft. It won't happen again."

"It certainly won't," she said slowly and deliberately.

What did she mean? That she wasn't allowed to take any more school trips? Or that she would no longer teach at the school? Sonia didn't ask. In the heat of the moment, Mrs. Ashcroft might say something that she would later regret. Brad had been a part of the school staff for years, but she was still on probation. If Mrs. Ashcroft decided that the two of them could not share that school, she'd be the one to go.

Pins pricked the back of her eyes. She needed that job. She couldn't knock on her parents' door and ask to be taken back until a knight on a white horse came to rescue her and make her his wife. His *house*wife. She couldn't end up like her mum.

After that call, Sonia couldn't sleep. With no TV, no books and her phone reminding her of the conversation she'd just had, she decided that the best thing to do was to leave her room and take a stroll in the garden. As she unclipped the chain on her door and remembered how she had locked herself in so that she wouldn't have the temptation to pop over to Brad's room, a wry smile curved her lips. Knocking on Brad's door was the last thing she'd do now that Mrs. Ashcroft had powerfully reminded her of the consequences.

How could I have not learned my lesson? After all that she had been through after a night with Callum, she should have known better. For goodness' sake, she wasn't sixteen anymore! And still, she'd been so stupid as to end up in bed with a colleague — and while they were on duty. She couldn't even blame it on the limoncello, because they hadn't had any the previous night. No, there was absolutely no danger that she would 'accidentally' bump into Brad's door on her way down to the garden.

It took Sonia's eyes some time to adjust to the low lighting of the moonless night. But when they did, stars exploded in the sky. Somebody was sitting on the bench where she had sat with Charlotte. A twig snapped under her feet and the shape on the bench turned around.

"Miss Alletti?" It was Charlotte's voice.

Sonia's breath caught in her throat. What was the girl doing out there at night again?

"Charlotte… Shouldn't you be in bed?"

"I waited till Laura was asleep before I sneaked out so that she wouldn't snitch on me." Even in the low light, Sonia could make out the grin on her face.

"Aren't you sleepy?"

"No. Neither are you," the girl said, as if she had been expecting Sonia to turn up. Suddenly it dawned on Sonia that what she had considered chance encounters were regular appointments for Charlotte. Last night's migraine must have been an excuse to go looking for her after waiting in vain at the bench for who knew how long. *Poor mite.*

"You look sad tonight, Miss." Charlotte's hands shot to cover her mouth. "Oh. My. God. Has my mum complained to you about last night?"

"No." It would have been better if she had, instead of ringing Mrs. Ashcroft.

"Phew." She dropped her hands back to her lap.

"And how are you?"

"Mum finally told me the truth. Dad has left." Charlotte's voice broke at the end.

"I'm sorry." Sonia squeezed her shoulder. "You will pull through."

"I don't know."

"You will. Losing someone doesn't mean that we have to lose ourselves."

"Have you ever lost someone, Miss?"

"Yes, mostly through my own fault."

"Do you miss them?"

"Yes. But now I know that I can survive." Her throat tightened. She had survived losing Callum and her baby. Now she would survive losing Brad, because he had never been hers. He had told her that he was sorry about their kiss in the sea and he had written that he was sorry about making love to her. Nothing suggested that he might not have been sorry even during it. Sonia swallowed the lump in her throat. "Come on. Let's go back. It's time we both got some sleep. Tomorrow we have a lot of traveling to do."

* * * *

Brad wasn't sad to leave the hotel. As well as having absolutely no reception for his phone, the room where he had spent the night with Sonia was not the best place to start trying to forget her. They sat apart on the coach again, and Brad plugged himself into his Italian language podcast.

It was a long drive to the Etna volcano and the wide dual carriageway soon turned into a windy climb. Sonia looked ashen as she chewed her travel sickness gums, clutching a plastic bag as if her life was inside it. He wished he could massage her wrists to make her feel better but, when she'd planted her bag on the seat next to her and stretching her legs on top of it, she couldn't have made it any clearer that she wanted to sit on her own. So, Brad just had to be content with suffering for her from a distance.

When they finally reached their first stop, two thousand meters above sea level, the children spurted out of the coach like a fizzy drink from a shaken bottle, while Sonia staggered out, looking relieved and surprised to have survived.

The view of the Sicilian island stretching out on one side with the Ionian Sea on the other was spectacular, but Brad couldn't enjoy it. He had spotted the funicular waiting for them, and his heart went, once again, to Sonia.

Her eyes widened with horror when she saw the cabins dangling from their metal cables, like the clothes Sicilians hang out to dry on strings stretched between buildings across the street. What with the low oxygen, the crowded space of the cabin and her fear of altitude, she was bound to have an asthma attack. But Sonia couldn't stay behind. Their new accommodation was the mountain refuge at the top. Was there a way to get her up there that didn't require losing contact with the ground?

Brad urgently scanned the car park and spotted a four-wheel-drive Unimog minibus that looked like something out of the USSR. The driver might be willing to taxi Sonia up to the hotel if Brad secretly paid him the equivalent fare for a busload.

"Why don't you take the minibus up? Jake, Katie and I can manage the kids on our own on the funicular," he murmured to her. "You wouldn't like it."

She darted him a reproachful look. "I'm jolly well going."

"Have you got your inhaler?"

"I won't need it," she said defiantly, tilting her chin in the same way as she had done the night when things had unraveled.

He knew better than to push her. It would only make her more stubborn. All he could do was to make sure that he ended up in the same car as her, so that he would be able to help her if she needed it. They walked up to the boarding platform. As each car could only take six people and they were thirty-two, some of the children would have to travel without an adult, even if Brad didn't travel with Sonia.

Jake boarded the first cabin with five children and Katie did the same with the next car. When the third car swung in, Sonia gestured to Brad to go ahead, but he stubbornly refused to go ahead of her. She would never jump into the same car as him. So that car flew off with six children. Eighteen of their party had gone.

When the fourth car approached, Sonia repeated her invitation and Brad ignored her, so six children filled that car. Eight of them were left on the platform, and it didn't take Einstein to work out that whoever didn't make it into the fifth car would have to travel with one other person in the sixth car.

Given that Jake and Katie had chosen to travel in separate cars, the six remaining children must have assumed that Miss Alletti and Mr. Wilson would be traveling separately too, and whichever child didn't make it into the fifth car would be left to travel alone with one of the teachers in the sixth car. So, when the next car swung in and the doors clunked open, all the children tried to squeeze in, including Sonia, who must have worked out that, if she didn't get in, she'd have to travel alone with Brad.

On this occasion, Brad's big frame and wide shoulders were a disadvantage. He had to watch Sonia being whisked away under his eyes.

Instead of enjoying the view, all through the ascent, Brad kept his eyes fixed on Sonia's car.

"Mr. Wilson, are you afraid of heights?" his traveling companion asked him. The boy didn't seem too put out by having missed traveling with the others. Aidan was one of Brad's biggest fans.

"No. Are you?"

"No. I just thought you were, because you're staring at the car in front and you're not looking down."

"I see. No, thankfully I don't suffer from acrophobia, but Miss Alletti does. That's why I'm keeping an eye on that car." *Why am I telling him?*

"You like Miss Alletti, don't you?"

Brad shifted on the seat. "Who doesn't?" he said, trying to sound casual.

"But you like her more."

It wasn't a question, so Brad didn't answer.

He was greatly relieved when they got to the other end and he saw her walk out of the car in front a little ashen but safe and sound.

"Snow!" the kids shouted when they got out of the funicular station. Walls of compacted snow flanked a road that pushed upwards like a black river carved deep within high, white banks. "Can we play in the snow?"

"I'm sorry, no. We still need to get to the refuge where we're staying," Sonia replied.

"Are we going there on foot?" one of the kids asked.

"Unfortunately not." A Unimog minibus was waiting for them with a running engine. Thank goodness this time they would all fit into one vehicle and he could keep an eye on Sonia. The higher they climbed, the lower the oxygen in the air and the worse an asthma attack could potentially be. Brad ran a hand over his face and got ready for the last leg of the journey.

Chapter Thirteen

Her room had none of the luxuries of the honeymoon suite of the last hotel, but Sonia was back-tinglingly glad to lie on her bed. What with her travel sickness and her fear of heights, the journey there had been grueling torture and she'd been a turn away from emptying out her stomach on a number of occasions.

Even the smell and the sight of the wild boar sausages that had been served for supper hadn't helped her recover her appetite. Thankfully, the crater they were going to visit the next day was only a short Unimog drive away, and the rest of the trip would be all on foot. At the crater they would collect the rock samples for the school's geology collection, the children would fill in their science worksheets and she could tick off all of the trip's learning objectives. She would pat herself on the back and take everyone home safe and sound.

Only, she wasn't really going to pat herself on the back, was she? Not after what had happened with Brad and not now that Mrs. Ashcroft knew — or, at least, had strong reasons to suspect — and Sonia's job was on the line. Had she had harsh words with Brad too?

Probably not. The woman probably thought she'd been the one to seduce him. Why else would Mr. Wilson have stooped so low?

Today he tried to stop me from going on the funicular. He was worried for me. He was worried about her asthma only because he didn't want a medical emergency on his hands. *He tried to push his way into my car to help me if I was unwell.* He did it only so that the children wouldn't be alone with her gasping and goggling while she was having an asthma attack. There could be no doubt. The message he had scribbled for her while she had been obliviously asleep had made it exceptionally clear that what had happened on that night had been against his better judgment — and he totally regretted it.

Lying on her bed, she looked out through the skylight at the stars twinkling in the high sky. Away from the light pollution of the lowlands, the stars seemed to be shining brighter — or maybe the sky was particularly clear tonight. That must be why the room felt a little cold.

She tossed around and closed her eyes. One more night and they'd be flying home. She and Brad could return to barely nodding a greeting when they inevitably passed each other in the corridors and successfully avoiding each other the rest of the time. A pang of something she couldn't name squeezed her chest.

Maybe she was finally hungry. She'd had no food since lunch and she wasn't one to skip meals without suffering the consequences. There was no way she could sleep well on an empty stomach. She remembered a vending machine by the entrance. Even a packet of crisps would be better than a grumbling stomach. She swung out of bed, turned on her bedside light and threw on her dressing gown. She thought again. It was still only eleven-thirty and there'd still be people sitting by the fire downstairs. She pulled off her nightie and threw on a fleece and a pair of jeans, without bothering with bra, T-shirt or socks. Then she slipped into her trainers, picked up her wallet and was off.

* * * *

Brad couldn't sleep. First, he had worried about Sonia having another asthma attack all through the journey. Then, when they'd finally gotten there, he'd noticed that she hadn't eaten a single crumb at suppertime. While all that was normal for someone who suffered from motion sickness and acrophobia, it *wasn't* normal for him to worry like an overprotective parent. Actually, the word 'worry' didn't even start to describe his reaction. Distress. Fear. Terror that she'd die... Those were better descriptions.

It certainly wasn't the way a man would feel about a colleague, even if they'd had sex, however amazing the sex had been.

He clenched his fists. Even acknowledging how beautiful that night had been made him feel guilty. He didn't deserve to have beautiful things in his life again.

Turning onto his back, he peered through the skylight at the night sky. Only the darkness of a moonless night allowed the stars to shine. Only in the bleakness of pain did the constellations of the human heart take shape. Sonia was there, in his heart, like the

Northern Star. Whatever bound them — whether it was friendship or lust or something else — Brad could have no doubt that it shone bright.

God, they were colleagues! How would he handle this, whatever 'this' was? His heartbeat pounded in his ears. He needed to get up, pace, scream. He heaved himself out of bed, threw on a pair of jeans and a fleece and made for the door to let the cold night air soothe him and give him peace. But peace was not what he got.

He got Sonia.

She must have been walking past when he yanked the door open, because she jumped, showering the crisps from the bag in her hands onto the floor. At least she had recovered her appetite.

"Sorry," he blurted automatically.

"Well, well, if 'sorry' isn't your favorite word." A muscle twitched in her jaw.

"I must be making lots of mistakes." Something flashed across her eyes. Whatever it was, it wasn't good. Had he said something wrong? A barb of panic jabbed him. "Should I have said something else?"

She squatted and started picking up the spilled crisps. "How about saying nothing and helping to tidy up this mess?"

"Quite. Sorry." *Argh, I said it again.*

He squatted and swept all the remaining crisps off the floor into one hand. "Give me the rest. I'll throw them away in my room."

Reluctantly, she opened her hand and poured all her crisp crumbs into his. "I thought that men didn't pick up stuff from the floor."

Ah. This was what it was about — the dirty laundry he'd forgotten on the bathroom floor. "This man usually does, but sometimes gets distracted."

She cocked an eyebrow. "What kind of thing distracts him?"

You. "Fear of doing something wrong, for example."

Without breaking eye contact, she straightened her legs and stood. He followed her.

"I have a feeling that this man doesn't have a clue which things are wrong and which aren't," she said slowly, deliberately.

Dangerous topics. He should run to his room, shut the windows and doors and hide in bed. *Don't even think about eating the crisps.* He should not engage in this conversation. "Give me an example."

Sonia bit her lip. "Not being there the next morning. That's wrong, for example."

"I beg to differ. If the man can't trust himself not to do more damage, not being there the next morning is judicious, not wrong. Perhaps cowardly, but surely wise."

Fire whooshed in her eyes just as water filled them. "What more damage could you have done, Brad? Telling me that the most amazing night of my life was a mistake? That you regretted it so much that you couldn't even bear to file it under your 'one-night stands' folder? Your scribbled message told all that, plus anything else I might like to imagine on a sad day."

"That wasn't the damage I meant." *Stroking your cheeks and starting to kiss you all over again until there was no way I would leave that room without holding on to your hand to make sure you didn't escape me. Until I had fallen so deep inside you that I could no longer pull myself out. That kind of damage.*

"What was it, then?" There was exasperation in her voice and tears were spilling over her eyelashes.

What he would have given to dry them off with his lips, to pull her quivering body into his arms and hold her until her sun shone again. But it would be wrong, so he clenched his fists instead.

"The truth is that you're a lone wolf. And a wolf is not a pet dog," she said.

Maybe she was right and he *was* a lone wolf. "Wolves have feelings too."

"But they're hunters—"

"I'm not a hunter, Sonia."

"And killers."

That last word froze him. It was a blow under the belt. All her trying to convince him that Frances' death wasn't his fault had been a lie. She had just called him a murderer. "Nice one. Sharp and dark. Then I shall return to my den so that you can have safe passage." He didn't even look her in the eye. He just swiveled around and went back into his room.

Oh, God, what had she said? She hadn't meant that he had killed his girlfriend! Why hadn't she picked some other animal, one that wasn't a hunter and a predator? Or a plant? She could have said, *A porcupine is not a bunny*, or *A stinging nettle is not a lettuce.*

Instead, she had hurt Brad right where the wound was very much raw and very much open. She'd never forget the look on his face. It would haunt her dreams. She had disintegrated him with one most ill-chosen, most unfortunate word. Yes, she had been with him at that moment. It had stung when he'd said that their night together had been wrong, all that talk of damage. But she had never meant to refer to the accident.

In a daze, she took a couple of aimless steps down the corridor. She had royally messed up and there was nothing she could do about it, because she would not knock on his door unless the hotel was on fire. The last time she had knocked on his door, things had happened that had catapulted them both into this horrid mess.

At the squeaking of a door, Sonia's heart slammed against her ribcage. Brad was back, giving *her* the chance to say 'sorry' to him. Sonia whipped around but the door that was opening wasn't Brad's. It was Charlotte's.

"Miss Alletti! I was just going to call you," Laura Hardman said, looking relieved. She did a double-take at Sonia's crisp packet.

"Is everything okay?"

"I'm not sure. Charlotte went to the toilet half an hour ago and she hasn't come back. She's probably just gone for one of her wanders, but I want to lock our door and go to sleep."

"Have you checked if she's in the toilets?"

"She wasn't there. I think she might have gone for a walk, Miss. She was a little upset because tomorrow is our last day and she doesn't want to go home."

Oh, no! Maybe Charlotte had gone knocking on her door when she was downstairs stuffing her face with crisps. Gluttony instead of lust this time. Was there any of the cardinal sins that she wasn't guilty of? "Thank you, Laura. I'll look for her. You go to bed but don't lock your door. If Charlotte comes back, please ring me or ask Mr. Wilson to ring me. Mr. Wilson is in this room here and Mr. and Mrs. Jenkins are at the end of the corridor on the right."

Laura went back into her room and Sonia checked the toilets, just in case. Nobody there. *There's no need to panic. I've always found her in the end.* She stuffed her empty packet of crisps in the bin and went out again. If they'd been in the first hotel, she would have gone straight to 'their' bench in the garden, but here there was no obvious place for Charlotte to be. Instead of a citrus orchard, they were surrounded by jagged ravines of black obsidian. Sonia rushed downstairs. She checked the sitting room with the fire, the games room, the dining room and even the kitchen. No Charlotte. The front desk was unmanned, so she asked an older couple sitting by the fire if they'd seen a blonde twelve-year-old girl. They shot Sonia a reproachful glance and shook their heads.

Don't panic…yet. She could be in someone else's room, having a little party. Sonia ran upstairs and listened carefully behind every door. No voices, no giggling. A room party was highly unlikely, especially as Laura would have gone too. Unless… *Oh. My. God. Please, let her not be with Aidan.* Icy terror shattered Sonia's knees. As she tried to run to Aidan and James' room, she had to remind herself that, even if they were together, they were only twelve and at most they'd be kissing. *Hope.*

She knocked forcefully — once, twice, desperately — and eventually Aidan appeared at the door, sleepy-faced and startled by the corridor's light. "Is it morning already?" It wasn't the face of a boy who's been canoodling with a girl in his room.

"Sorry, Aidan. I was looking for Charlotte and I thought…er…that she might have told you where she was going."

"Charlotte is missing?" That piece of information seemed to have instantly woken him.

"Don't worry. I'm sure I'll find her in one of the other girls' rooms. Go to bed. Sorry to have disturbed you."

"Miss… Do you think you could let me know when you find her? Don't worry about waking me…because I don't think I'll be able to go back to sleep."

"I will, Aidan. But do try to sleep now. I'm sure she's fine. She's probably just out by the entrance watching the stars." Sonia felt her heart thaw a little at the boy's expression.

Right, so Charlotte was not in the refuge. *Time to panic.* Sonia's eyes shot to Brad's door. *You must tell him.* If she told him, he would insist on going out to look for her while she stayed in the refuge and called the emergency services. *You don't want to tell him because you're ashamed.* Yes, that was also a reason.

She was ashamed at having called him a killer and ashamed of having let Charlotte slip under her radar, again. She should have sensed that things were not well with her when she did her night rounds. She should have anticipated that the end of the trip would be difficult for Charlotte. But that was only the tip of her iceberg of shame. She had failed her own baby. She was incapable of doing good and she should not be trusted. She should have told Charlotte's mum that she was putting her hopes in the wrong person. If anything happened to Charlotte tonight, it would be *her* fault. *But you've got to tell him.* Sonia swallowed and knocked hard on that door.

Brad opened the door a crack, as if he wasn't sure whether he wanted to see her.

"Hi." An irresistible urge to torture her bottom lip took her over. "I'm really sorry about what I said earlier. I didn't realize how it sounded until the words were already out." *There, the hardest part is out.* She took a breath and continued.

"The second thing is that I can't find Charlotte Rogers. She's not in her room or anywhere in the refuge, as far as I can see. I'm going to have a little walk out, not far, just to check that she's not sitting on a boulder watching the stars. But I thought I'd let you know before I went out. If I don't come back with her very soon, I think that you should call the emergency services."

"I'll go. You stay."

He made to leave the room but she placed a hand on his chest to stop him. "Sorry, Brad, but I need to do this. I was personally entrusted with Charlotte by her mother. It's my duty. But I've got my phone on me, so call me if she comes back in the meantime."

"Don't go far, Sonia. Please."

"I won't. Don't worry," she shouted back, halfway down the corridor. Thankfully, 'far' was an unquantifiable amount.

A handful of scraggy gnarled trees broke the uniformity of a landscape that was entirely made of tufts of hardy grasses and expanses of ash so black and so matte that it sucked in even that little light given off by the stars. Sonia squinted, trying to adjust her vision, and hoped that Charlotte was wearing her red cardigan.

"Charlotte?" she called. She imagined her voice rolling off the edges, down into the craggy ravines. There was no reply. But her phone rang.

"Hello?"

"Miss?" It was Charlotte's voice. Sonia's heart went into overdrive.

"Where are you?"

"I'm not sure…" The whistling of wind at the other end told her that Charlotte was not indoors, and Sonia felt like a ball of lead had materialized in her throat.

"Are you okay?"

"I can't walk. My ankle hurts too much," the girl whimpered.

The lead ball sank down to Sonia's stomach. "Where are you? How did you get there?"

"I walked out and went straight up until I got to a crater and there I…slipped into it."

Maybe it hadn't been an accidental slip. "Stay there—" *Duh*! "I'm on my way. See if you can share your location with me from your phone."

As soon as she hung up, Sonia rang Brad but there was no answer. So she turned on her phone's torch and set off at a very brisk pace toward the looming dark peak straight in front of her.

* * * *

As soon as he was off the phone with the emergency services, Brad knocked on Jake and Katie's door and told them what was happening. They offered to watch over the kids if he wanted to join Sonia in the search, which was exactly what he intended to do.

Then he rushed back to his room, grabbed his phone and the first-aid kit and was about to leave when he noticed a missed call from Sonia. He rang back.

"Have you found her?"

"Sort of." Sonia's heavy breathing and the rustling of wind gave him a frisson of fear. "She's slipped into the crater that is straight up from the refuge. This is a good time to call the emergency services."

"Already done. Where are you?"

"On my way to the crater," she said, as if it should be obvious.

Brad's whole body tightened. Sonia was scrambling up a craggy mountain of lava at night. "I don't think you should."

"She sounded distressed. I know where she is. She shared her location." Her tone suggested that arguing wouldn't achieve anything other than tiring everyone out. He'd just have to get to her before the sulfurous gases, the darkness and the uneven, unfamiliar terrain got her into trouble. Just the thought that something bad could happen to her was enough to churn Brad's insides.

"Please, send me her location so I can pass it to the mountain rescue people."

"Good thinking."

On his way out, he dropped by her room — luckily, she had left it unlocked — and got her inhaler. Now all he needed was a Unimog to get to Sonia and Charlotte before it was too late.

Six of them were parked outside, but they were all locked. There was no one around to ask for the keys — all the lights were off, everyone in bed. But parked just by the entrance, with the keys left in the ignition, was a motorbike.

Don't even think about it.

The owner must have decided that no thief would be crazy enough to ride off with it on that road. It wasn't really a road, more of a dirt track of fresh, sharp volcanic gravel. Still, someone must have ridden it up there.

The last time I rode a motorbike, I killed a person and almost killed myself too.

And he didn't even have a helmet. But Charlotte was stranded in a crater, in distress, and Sonia was bound to have an asthma attack with all the stress, the physical exertion and the volcanic fumes. Hell, he had to get to them as fast as he could, even if the idea of riding that motorbike up that gravel track in the pitch black made him retch.

He dug his nails into his palms. Then he clasped the handlebar, swung his right leg over the saddle and turned on the ignition.

* * * *

If she hadn't known that hydrogen sulfide smelled like rotten eggs, she would have thought that the desolate landscape around her was an open-air rubbish dump. Still, if the veil that shrouded the stars wasn't low-lying clouds but steam and sulfuric gases, she must be getting close to the edge of the crater. She took a lungful of stinky air and shouted Charlotte's name, but there was no answer other than her own cough.

Charlotte's mother's words played in her head. *'I caught her watching a teen suicide video.'* Why else would Charlotte have scrambled all the way up there in the middle of the night through that noxious smell, if not to…? Sonia shuddered and her eyes prickled with tears. Maybe it was because of the gases. She took a deep breath — *why is it so damn hard to breathe?* — before calling Charlotte's name again.

She thought she heard someone call 'Miss', but either Charlotte's voice was very feeble or very far — or the sound was only the whistling of the wind.

"Charlotte, where are you?"

"Down here." It was faint but definitely not the wind.

Sonia scanned the crater with her phone's torch but its light was almost as feeble as Charlotte's voice. Maybe the battery was running out or the cloud was too thick. She carried on climbing until she had managed to pick out a splash of red halfway down the crater.

"Stay there. I'm coming!"

That red dot must be the cardigan she had lent Charlotte on the airplane. *'I like to keep an eye on my clothes,'* she had told Charlotte days ago. The fact that the girl still hadn't returned her things couldn't be anything but a plea to Sonia to keep watch over her, which Sonia had epically failed to do. But this was her chance to put things right.

Sonia climbed over the ridge and started scrambling down into the crater. Her eyes, nose and throat stung. How could Charlotte bear it? "Hold on tight. I'm coming!"

The torch could only light a few steps ahead of her feet, which was all the better, because Sonia didn't have any desire to see how steep the ground was, or how far away was the bottom of the crater. With every step, her feet sank into the ash and she slipped a little farther down than she had expected. Getting back up would be as hard as climbing a sand dune. Every now and then she pointed the torch in Charlotte's direction, each time struggling to locate the red cardigan. When she finally reached the girl, Sonia's eyes were streaming and burning like she'd had an onion eye mask.

"It's okay. I'm with you. The emergency services are on their way."

"I think I've broken my leg. I can't move it," Charlotte whimpered through chattering teeth.

"We've got to get you out of here. These fumes aren't good for you." Sonia had long been feeling an ominous and familiar tingling in her throat, but she had decided to ignore it. She had stupidly left her inhaler in the room, of course. She passed her phone to Charlotte. "Point the torch in front of us as I carry you."

"Miss, you can't. I'm heavy."

"I'm stronger than I look." Sonia was trying to convince herself as much as Charlotte. "Grab on to my shoulders." Sonia turned around and Charlotte wrapped her arms around Sonia's neck, triggering a bout of coughing.

"Sorry, Miss."

"My shoulders, not my throat." There was already enough tightening and clenching going on in that part of her body.

Charlotte shifted her hands and Sonia hitched her legs around her waist as best she could without losing her balance. Her thighs burned as each step slipped back, sending a cascade of small stones rolling down into the pit. Her lungs felt as full as two shriveled dried cherries. Each breath—*gasp*—was insufficient and unsatisfying but the more she breathed, the more her throat stung. It felt like when fizzy water went into her nose. She wanted to ask Charlotte a million questions, like how and why she had gotten up there, but she couldn't spare a wisp of breath. And Charlotte had started coughing too.

A helicopter roared in the distance with its searchlight frantically sweeping the ragged slopes.

"Flash the torch at them," Sonia wheezed to Charlotte.

Now that she knew help had arrived, the extraordinary strength that had allowed her to carry Charlotte halfway up the crater instantly drained away. She might just about make it out of the crater without Charlotte on her back, but not under the girl's weight. The helicopter was still far and her lungs were screaming to get the hell out of there, but she'd rather suffocate to death than leave Charlotte behind. *God, help us.*

Her head seemed clamped in an invisible vise that had started to spin. Her eyes and throat stung like raw acid. Her lungs were like vacuum bags. But she pushed on, until her hearing became muffled, her thinking muddled and her vision so blurred that she didn't see the flickering light scrambling down the crater toward them. When her eyelids started to inescapably descend over her eyes, Sonia resigned herself to death. Even if it'd be a shame never to be in Brad's arms again, taste one of his kisses or smell the scent of his skin.

A real shame.

And she collapsed.

Chapter Fourteen

The moment Brad saw that little torchlight quivering slowly up the crater, he knew that he'd found them. But it was only after he'd stopped the motorbike and started scrambling down the the slippery side that he realized — with horror — that Sonia was carrying Charlotte on her shoulders up the fuming crater.

"Sonia! Charlotte!" he roared over the sound of the helicopter's blades that were churning the air, not too far away now.

Charlotte waved her arms. Sonia didn't. Brad saw her crumple — gradually, jerkily, as if each one of her limbs was fighting a solo battle to stay up. As she sank to the ashy ground, Brad's heart sank to the place where only hot magma existed. A roar of rage and desperation erupted from his throat as he felt a fissure crack right through him. No man could be torn away from both the women he had loved and survive. Yes, he loved Sonia. He loved her as much as he had loved Frances — and a whole heap more.

He almost free-fell down the slope, heedless of whether he'd live or die. He was desperate to reach the woman he loved more than life.

He scooped Sonia up from the ashes and hitched her up onto his shoulders, holding her securely with one arm in a fireman's carry. With the other arm he picked up Charlotte and, breathing hard and fast with the effort and the fear of losing Sonia, he clambered up the slope. Big mouthfuls of the noxious gases seared his insides, but he didn't slow down. When his thighs were on fire and his eyes and throat felt like raw wounds, he pressed on. There was no part of him that didn't feel like an open wound.

By the time he reached the rim of the crater, the mountain rescue team had landed with stretchers and oxygen masks. They immediately took care of Charlotte, but Brad insisted on looking after Sonia himself. "Don't give in, Sonia. Don't do that to me," he whispered into her ear until the oxygen made her eyes flutter open again.

By now, tears were streaming down Brad's cheeks, and they weren't caused by the volcanic gases. She smiled and it was like the sun was rising again. The million things he wanted to tell her got jammed in his throat. Instead, he looked into her beautiful eyes and, stupefied with joy, he wrapped her hand in his and kissed it.

She tried to say something but the oxygen mask swallowed her words. Brad didn't care. She was alive.

He went up in the helicopter with Sonia and Charlotte and spent the night at the hospital, watching over them, even after they'd fallen asleep.

The following morning, at the first lights of dawn, he hired a taxi back to the funicular station then a

Unimog up to the crater where he had left the motorbike. The Unimog driver was very surprised that he had ridden a motorbike all the way up there. Riding back was much easier in the light. He would have to apologize and thank the owner profusely.

When he parked at the entrance of the refuge, a voice called down to him from a window.

"Mr. Wilson, has Miss Alletti found Charlotte?" It was Aidan.

"Yes."

"Is she all right?"

Brad recognized that keen concern that comes with a special affection, and his heart went out to the boy. "She's fine. Very nice people are looking after her." Then he went inside and straight up to Jake and Katie to tell them everything that had happened.

* * * *

The image of the tense lines in Brad's face scattering into a smile played in Sonia's mind on a loop. When her world had gone blacker than basalt and she had believed that it was the end, she had woken up to find Brad by her side. He'd been there for her when she'd needed him. *As always.*

"Your friend has asked me to tell you that he's gone back to the refuge," the nurse told her, "but he will come back to collect you when we discharge you."

Before, Sonia would have told the nurse that Brad was a colleague, not a friend. But now she didn't, because it wasn't true. She didn't know how he had managed to be there when she had opened her eyes again after what she'd thought to be her last time closing them, but she had the feeling that he'd spent the night by her bedside. That the hand offering her sips of water every time she surfaced from her sleep was his.

As soon as the nurse was gone, Charlotte called from her bed, "Are you awake, Miss Alletti?"

"Yes. How are you, Charlotte?"

Charlotte gave her a very-sorry-puppy look. "I'm really very, very sorry, Miss. Thank you for coming to look for me."

"It was my duty. I promised your mum that I'd keep a special eye on you."

A cloud fell over Charlotte's face. "Mum is the reason why I was there last night. We had an argument—a pretty bad one. I couldn't see how I could go back home and live with her again, so I thought of…killing myself by jumping into a crater full of lava. But there was no lava, only spiky gravel."

"I'm mighty glad that there was no lava—and that you rang me and told me where you were. I hope you never feel like that again but, if you should, please, come and talk to me before doing anything silly," Sonia told her.

"I will, Miss."

"Ah, I just remembered something that might make you think twice before doing anything like jumping into craters again. I knocked on Aidan's door last night—"

Sonia could almost see Charlotte's ears prick up.

"In case he knew where you might be. As soon as he heard that you were missing, he looked worried sick."

"Really?"

"Uh-huh. Please, send him a text if your phone has any battery power. He made me promise to let him know when I found you."

Just then, a lovely lady doctor walked in and smiled at Charlotte. "Well, well, well… I don't know what you and your mum were doing up in that crater in the middle of the night," she said in English, "but you're very lucky to be still alive."

Sonia's chest tingled at the word 'mum'.

"No, Miss Alletti is my teacher. She's way too young to be my mum."

"Of course she's too young. Sorry. It's just that the man who was with you told the paramedics that she carried you out of the crater on her back, so I assumed that she must be your mum. A little longer in that crater and you two would both have been poisoned by the volcanic gases." Then she turned to Sonia. "You must love your students very much, because what you did was very dangerous for someone with asthma."

"Miss, you have asthma? You could have died for me!"

The doctor turned to Charlotte again. "Volcanic gases are full of hydrogen sulfide, which is heavier than air, so it sinks in the crater. The concentration down there must have been extremely high. Yes, your teacher risked her life for you."

Sonia's heart soared. She had saved Charlotte's life. Hot, fat tears bubbled from her eyes and flopped onto the oxygen tubes. Maybe she had killed her baby girl, but now she had saved Charlotte's life.

"So did the man who was with you, who carried you both up, according to the paramedics' report," the doctor added.

Man who carried us both up? "Who was that?" Sonia asked. Hadn't the paramedics carried them up on stretchers?

218

"Miss, it was Mr. Wilson," Charlotte replied enthusiastically. "He put you on his shoulder and grabbed me with one arm. Then he climbed, puffing and panting, all the way up."

Sonia's tears became a waterfall as the pressure of emotions erupted from her chest. She didn't deserve a crumb of the thing Brad had done for her. She wasn't worth a button of his T-shirt. And it all felt too much.

* * * *

Despite Jake and Katie's offer to take the kids on the guided excursion to the crater without him, Brad insisted on joining them. He was their science teacher and it was his duty to go. Even if he'd had enough of craters, he'd had no sleep, and he was on tenterhooks to hear any news of Sonia and Charlotte from the hospital.

The guide took them to a different crater from the one Brad had 'visited' because, in that one, the slopes were too steep and the volcanic gases too concentrated. They collected the rock samples, filled in their worksheets and did all that they were meant to do. But the kids were unusually subdued. They must have been worried for Sonia and Charlotte too.

On the way back in the Unimog, he sat next to Laura, whose usual sitting partner was missing.

"Don't be sad, Laura. A fractured leg is not the end of the world. Charlotte will recover very soon."

"I know. I'm just sad that the trip is almost over."

"But we'll see each other again in school in a week's time."

"But it won't be the same, Mr. Wilson. You won't be playing football with us, eating with us, playing Truth or... Truth with us. It'll be lessons, homework, detentions... Everything will go back to like it was before."

'Everything will go back to like it was before.' Yes, once the trip was over, there would be no chance or reason for all the things Laura had mentioned — no reason for Sonia and him to spend time together. But he couldn't let her slip away! Last night, when he'd thought that he was losing her forever, he had realized how much she meant to him.

She had reawakened his heart, rescued him from grieving and from the gray, flickering existence he had been half-living since the accident. She had injected color into his world and pulled him out of his darkness. He hadn't rescued her. She had rescued him.

When he had pulled her out of the crater, not caring whether he lived or died, he had discovered that he loved her. She had cracked him down the middle and made him whole again. At that point, for the first time since the accident, he felt that his debt had been repaid. He had found redemption and was allowed to be happy again.

No, he couldn't let Sonia slip away from him. He wanted to spend the rest of his life with her, have children with her, grow old with her...if she wanted to. Oh God, how he hoped that she wanted to!

"Thank you, Laura."

"What for?"

"For making me see things clearly."

Laura shrugged.

When the Unimog trundled over the hump and into the refuge's car park, two figures were standing by the entrance — one on crutches, the other...just lovely. Brad's heart swelled with hope as he imagined Sonia standing at the door of a home that they shared, next to their children. In a few hours, this trip would be over and they'd be flung back to lives that only brushed past each other in the school corridors. No, he couldn't bear it. He must talk to her before he lost her forever.

* * * *

Despite the souvenirs she had bought and her ceramic plate, which had just been delivered, there was still space in Sonia's suitcase. Something must be missing, but what? *It's the piece of my heart that Brad has taken with him.* Nonsense!

Someone knocked on the door and Sonia went to open it.

"Hi, Miss. Thank you for the clothes. You can have them back now." Charlotte was balancing on her crutches, holding Sonia's red cardigan and her jeans.

"I had completely forgotten about them."

"No, you hadn't, Miss. You've been keeping an eye over them all this time."

"Not always as well as I would have liked to. I'm sorry."

"Don't say that. You've been wonderful, Miss!" Charlotte dropped the clothes and crutches and tipped herself forward onto Sonia to hug her.

Sonia's heart swelled as Charlotte whispered against her chest, "Thank you, Miss."

"My duty…and pleasure."

"Er…Miss? I'm kind of stuck. Could you help me pick up my crutches?"

At that, they both burst into laughter.

When Charlotte had left, Sonia packed the clothes into her suitcase. The next time she wore them, she would surely feel like Charlotte was hugging her again. Then she washed her face, changed into clean clothes and put up her hair, ready for dinner.

That evening's meal was a subdued affair, despite the fact that the cook seemed to have gone the extra mile for their last meal at the refuge. Sonia had never eaten a pistachio pesto as good as the one they were served or an escalope so soft. She was preparing a speech to thank the refuge staff in her head when all the lights in the dining room suddenly went off and everyone gasped.

As they were plunged into darkness and silence, a faint fizzing and crackling noise coming from the kitchen grew louder. A flickering light glowed brighter and brighter through the glass of the kitchen doors until they burst open, and a spluttering sparkler lit the room and the volcano-shaped cake on which it was planted.

"Oooh!" went the kids, and the chef's Cheshire Cat smile was illuminated from below by the sparkler.

"Thhis is the chef's special for your last supper with us — the Etna cake!" he announced proudly.

Aidan whooped, everyone clapped and the man put the cake down in front of Sonia and wiped his hands on the apron tucked under his blooming belly.

Then someone switched the lights back on and the cake appeared in all its spongy and crusty splendor. It was a mound as black as the darkest chocolate and it was surrounded by a miniature fence of red, purple, orange and yellow slices of prickly pear.

"Will you do me the honor of cutting the cake, *Professoressa*?" The chef offered Sonia the knife.

"Of course." Sonia cracked the chocolate crust and dug the knife through the soft sponge underneath.

Everyone oohed when dark chocolate oozed out of the hot, melted core.

"We want this for our school dinners, Mr. Jenkins!" Ryan shouted.

Jake immediately whipped out his phone and took a photo.

"Try dipping the prickly pear slices in the chocolate," the chef recommended when everyone had been served their portion.

"Have you taken out all the spines from the prickly pears?" Hazel asked suspiciously.

"Of course…after soaking them overnight." Then, as a demonstration—or maybe it was just an excuse to try some—the man picked a slice of prickly pear, dipped it generously in the chocolate lava and popped it in his mouth.

Everyone immediately copied him. It was such a pleasure seeing the kids enjoying their last evening in Sicily. Feeling a little emotional, she stood up and tinkled a fork on her glass. "I'm sure that I'm not the only one here who would like to thank all the refuge staff for their hospitality. They've really done their best to make our stay here as comfortable and enjoyable as possible. We also need to thank Mr. and Mrs. Jenkins, who agreed to spend a very crowded honeymoon so that we could all go on this trip. And Mr. Wilson, who stepped in with no notice and saved the day—as he seems to do very often. Thank you, Mr. Wilson." Her voice cracked and she didn't trust herself to even glance at him without betraying the emotions that were cavorting in her heart. "And thank you, Year Sevens, for being such fun to travel with. I'm sure that each of us will remember something different about this trip, but I hope that everyone will remember this adventure for years to come and that at least some of it will end up in your treasured memories chest. Mostly, I hope that you'll always remember what it feels like to be a visitor in a foreign country and how nice it is to feel welcome, so that you will be welcoming to strangers too."

Everyone lifted their Coca-Colas and Fantas and cheered.

As soon as Sonia sat down, Aidan stood.

"Miss Alletti, we want to thank you for this trip too. You worked the hardest of everyone. We have a little something for you and Mr. Wilson and Mr. and Mrs. Jenkins."

There was some fumbling under the table and some shifting of chairs, then two flat, round parcels traveled from hand to hand until one reached Sonia and the other landed on Jake's lap.

Sonia felt her throat knot up and her eyes tingle. She wasn't expecting a present at all. It was so sweet that the kids had got together to organize presents, and she felt so touched that she didn't notice that there were only two packets. Sonia had already started to rip the paper when Charlotte called out, "Wait, Miss Alletti. You have to open it with Mr. Wilson. It's for both of you."

A present for sharing? She glanced at Brad and saw in his face the same heart-fluttering surprise that she felt in hers. Meanwhile, Jake and Katie were making good progress against the reels of tape that bound their parcel like a cage by hacking it with one of the meat knives off the table.

"Wow, kids, this is fantastic!" Jake pulled out a ceramic plate. It was covered in the kids' signatures and at the center, in beautiful calligraphy, someone had written *To Mr. and Mrs. Jenkins* against the backdrop of a red heart.

"We made it at the ceramic workshop," Hazel said.

"And none of you noticed!" Ryan said.

"This is better than any of our wedding presents," Katie said with glittering eyes.

"Miss Alletti and Mr. Wilson! Open your present," Charlotte called. "I painted yours!"

Sonia felt a tinge of panic. What if Charlotte had painted a heart on their plate too? It wouldn't be unlike her to do things without thinking of the consequences. Sonia shuddered at the thought of Mrs. Ashcroft seeing it.

"Mr. Wilson, open it!" Aidan called.

Brad got up slowly, looking as reluctant as Sonia felt. They stripped the parcel from opposite ends, both with trembling fingers. At the sight of a speck of red, Sonia swallowed. Brad ripped the paper right across and… No, it wasn't a heart! It was a red starfish!

Sonia remembered the starfish in the seagrass meadow when Brad had saved her life the first time. Charlotte couldn't have known. Nobody knew, not even Brad, who had dived into the water only after she had started swimming back up. It was either chance or…one of those inexplicable things that connect heaven and earth.

"It's a starfish," Charlotte explained, "because you and Mr. Wilson have enough arms to love everybody, like a starfish. At first I thought of painting an octopus but an octopus is gray and that color doesn't suit you. You are more like red."

Sonia opened her mouth to say thank you but, instead of words, a strangled sob came out. Brad immediately wrapped an arm around her waist. *Of course*. He was always there by her side when she needed him.

"Thank you, Charlotte, and thank you, everyone," Brad said, sparing Sonia the difficulty of speaking without crying. "Now, who wants seconds?"

"Me!"

"Me!"

"Me!"

Brad took over the distribution of the remainder of the cake with mathematical precision while Jake scuttled to the kitchen to ask the chef nicely for the recipe. Katie and Sonia wrapped the plates back in the paper.

When the meal was over, as everyone was going upstairs to finish packing, Sonia stopped Brad. However much she wanted to keep the plate, Brad had the same right. Surely they could come to some kind of 'custody' agreement and keep it in the languages office and in the science office on a rota. "What would you like to do about this? I have space in my suitcase, if you'd like me to carry it, but when we get back, we will share it, of course."

"You should have it. Charlotte painted it and you went into the crater for her."

"But you pulled both of us out. If you hadn't, I don't think that I would have made it out alive. I have no idea how I can ever thank you enough —"

"I do."

"And I'm still totally baffled by how you managed to reach us so quickly." Had he just said that he had an idea of how she could thank him? Sonia wished that her tongue hadn't been faster than her brain, because now it was too late to ask him.

"I 'borrowed' the motorbike that's parked by the entrance." He grinned.

"Do you still ride? I mean, after the accident?"

Sonia noticed that he didn't wince at her last word.

"No. Last night was the first time."

"Oh, Brad!" She felt like throwing her arms around him but stopped herself as there were still people in the room. "It must have been so hard to get on a bike again, in the pitch black, on a nonexistent track. You must have been terrified."

"Not as much as I was terrified of…" His voice trailed off and his gaze flitted to Jake, who was walking out of the kitchen.

"Sonia, Brad, here you are." He planted himself in front of them and looked at them sternly. "The two of you have had a hell of a night, so I'll be very cross if you refuse to let me and Katie put the kids to bed and be on duty tonight." He whipped three big Post-it notes out of his back pocket. The first two read *Do Not Disturb*, while the third one read *If You're Upset, Can't Sleep, are Unwell, Want to Weep, Too Sad or Gripped with Fear, Bring All of Your S**t to Jake and Katie Here!*

Brad gave a deep throaty laugh that made Sonia's insides melt. "Are you for real, man?"

"Of course."

Then he looked Jake straight in the eyes. "Have you ever thought of moving out of the kitchen and into a classroom? You'd make a darn good teacher, I reckon."

"Maybe. First, let's see how tonight goes. Now I'm going to slap these two on your doors and this one on ours. See you in the morning."

"Thank you, Jake. You are a sweetie." Sonia wasn't so much looking forward to an uninterrupted night's sleep—although she badly needed one—but to a few minutes' undisturbed time with Brad. Maybe, if the kids were being looked after by Jake and Katie, she could have a little heart-to-heart talk with him. The next day, they'd be back home and she needed to know how she should behave. Whether the fact that he'd saved her life counted for something or whether they'd go back to nodding a greeting when they crossed in the corridors, she needed to know.

Yes, because she had fallen in love with Brad Wilson. Denying it would be like burying her head in the sand — or, as she had done in Mondello, dunking it into the sea. Eventually, she would have to surface again, gasping and loving even more than before.

She would never be able to break free of loving him until he rejected her — unequivocally, terminally, the most brutally the better. His 'sorry' note had been a good start, but the volcano rescue had confused everything again. The way he had circled her waist when she had been about to break into tears about the plate — as if he could tell, even without seeing her face — hadn't helped either. It had made her wish that he was there to stay, hers to keep and to wake up next to every morning.

Dangerous wish.

If colleagues or, at most, friends was all they could ever be, she needed to know. They needed to talk. Tonight.

That was why, when Jake had left and Brad asked her if she wanted to go for a stroll, she immediately accepted. But it was only when he pulled his phone out of his pocket and switched it onto 'Do not disturb' mode that she realized that he wanted to talk to her too. Her heart slammed against her ribcage.

As they walked out of the entrance and around the back of the building, where a little garden of succulent alpine plants hugged the stones, they didn't say a word. The stars had started to twinkle in the clear sky and the view that stretched over the Ionian Sea on the left and the green plains on the right was breathtaking, not that she needed anything to take her breath away. Brad was more than enough.

As they carried on walking, the rockery of high-altitude species turned into something a little wilder, with tufts of pink *Saponaria sicula* in bloom and exuberant yellow bushes of *ginestra*, Etna's Scotch broom.

Sonia couldn't tell if the swell of emotion in her chest was about the landscape or about the man next to her.

Brad stopped to smell some *ginestra*.

"Wow, how many insects are buzzing around these flowers?" she exclaimed, unable to broach the topic that was really pressing inside her heart.

Brad straightened. "A scientist once said that, judging by their abundance, the Creator must have an inordinate fondness for stars and beetles."

"Quite." She turned and looked into the depths of his emerald eyes. "And you? Do you have any inordinate fondness — ?"

"As a matter of fact, I do." He tossed his head back and closed his eyes.

Then he opened them again and looked at her. Her heart was beating so hard that it felt like it would jump right through her ribs. She saw in Brad's pupils the same wish that burned in her chest. The same hope. The same longing.

The night before, in the crater, when she had seen the end of her road, her coffin gaping open, she had wished to be in his arms one more time. When darkness had been deepest, she had seen her heart clearly.

She didn't care if loving Brad meant that she'd lose her job. She didn't give a toss if she ended up spending her days at the stove with varicose veins bulging out of her legs like her mum. She didn't care if she had to pick up endless dirty laundry from every floor of the house while Brad went off to do his high-flying surgeon job. She would bear all that, if needed, rather than be without him even just one day, so long as every night she could fall asleep wrapped in his arms and wake up in the morning to the smile that made her heart flip upside down and inside out. But she didn't deserve him.

Very few people in this world deserve anything. All the rest of us must accept what we're given and be grateful, she had told him once. Now she needed to tell herself — and believe it. After all, he had risked life and limb for her, so she must be worth something, at least to him. And, *to him* was all that mattered to her.

The air between them started singing as he took her hands and placed them on his chest. She could feel his heart, strong and fast, under her palms. He gave a long sigh. "I have an inordinate fondness for you."

A little whimper escaped her throat.

"You're not made of sugar, spice and all things nice. You're made of light, joy and slices of paradise." He gave her a look so intense that the air between them crackled. "I love you, Sonia," he croaked.

"I love you too, Brad."

He pulled something out of his jacket pocket and handed it to her. "When Giovanna said that we should paint what makes us happy, I could only think of you.

This is for you—a memory of our night on the balcony drinking limoncello."

She unwrapped the parcel. It was the plate he had painted with the view from the balcony. "And I painted the sea where we met underwater."

Then he pulled her to his chest and lowered his mouth onto hers. He kissed her softly, tenderly, as if she was the most precious thing in the world. All her five senses, plus some more she didn't know she had, became filled with Brad. Everything else around them stopped existing. There, in his arms, she felt like she was finally home.

Then he pulled away and looked into her eyes. She saw a man barely holding himself together. "I want you like I've never wanted any other woman."

"But will you be sorry in the morning?" she murmured.

"The only thing I'll ever be sorry about would be if I ever was stupid enough to let you go."

"That's good, because I don't want to go anywhere—not without you."

He took her hand and led her to a patch of soft ash and lapilli behind the ginestra bush. He pulled off his jacket and laid it down on the ground. A pantheon of stars twinkled above them, brighter than ever, as they were far from the lights of the cities.

Sonia lay down on Brad's jacket. It smelled of him and that unsettled her a little more, especially when he lay down next to her.

"Do Italians just dine *al fresco* or do they do…other things *al fresco* too?" he asked, staring at the starry sky above them.

"What sort of things?" she asked, even though she knew the answer.

"Things like this." He rolled onto his side and kissed her again, softly and tenderly.

It was like the last little tug needed to unravel a bow. "I won't be able to be responsible for my actions if you kiss me like that, Mr. Wilson."

"You have no one to answer to, Miss Alletti. The stars are winking, the breeze is singing and the volcano has provided us a warm, soft bed."

She wrapped her arms around his neck. "You make me wicked, Mr. Wilson."

He slipped his hands under her top. "I'd rather have a wicked you than a good other woman," he whispered into her ear, sending a frisson of excitement all over her body.

That night, on the searing hot volcano, they let their love flow like lava and melted into each other under an eruption of stars.

Epilogue

Sonia packed her bag for the umpteenth time. *Laptop, check. Lesson props, check. Timetable, check.* She shouldn't feel butterflies in her stomach. It wasn't like this was her first day in a new school. She was returning to her old classes, the kids she knew and loved, just one year older. And they loved her now just as much as they'd done before, judging by the lovely pressies they had made in DT lessons for baby Emma — her and Brad's 'Made in Sicily' baby. So much for her conviction that she was unable to have children.

Staring at the blue lines on the little white stick, her emotion had overflowed into tears of distilled happiness. Brad had been just as excited and had immediately started planning the nursery. Her wedding dress had been empire-waisted out of necessity, but it was very elegant and beautiful, and even her mum and dad had not been able to resist Brad's charm and had refrained from calling their wedding a *matrimonio riparatore,* a 'reparation wedding'.

Her life was perfect, and there was no reason to be nervous about anything, least of all about returning to work after her maternity leave.

Brad appeared on the threshold, cradling baby Emma and smiling. "You look gorgeous."

She had chosen one of the flowery dresses she had worn in Sicily. "Thank you."

"Are you all packed and ready?"

"I think so."

"Emma and I will be off to the botanic gardens. I'll send you pics, if you promise not to be jealous." He flashed her a cheeky grin. "And don't worry. I won't take her to the scary human anatomy museum…yet."

She looked at Emma and her heart gave a little squeeze. It was the first time she would be away from her child for so many hours. Her nerves were nothing to do with returning to the classroom, which she loved. Really, they were about leaving Emma.

Back in the days when she thought that marriage and motherhood would chain her doubly to the kitchen sink like her mum, she would never have believed that a day would come when being at home with a baby would feel like a blessing instead of a conviction. But she still loved her job and her 'other children', her students. They were waiting for her and she was looking forward to teaching them again.

Her phone rang in her bag and she picked it up.

"Mamma, you've learned how to make a videocall!"

"Of course! I want to see my baby *nipotina*!"

"That's great, but you need to switch your camera around, or we'll only ever see your feet."

"Oh, never mind me. Show me Emma."

Sonia tilted the screen toward Emma and Brad, and a squeal came out of the phone as her mum cooed over her grandchild.

"I've got to go now, Mamma."

"Well, I actually rang to wish you a good day."

Sonia felt a tingle of pleasure. "Thank you."

"*Figlia mia*, you are so lucky to have found a man who lets you go to work while he stays at home," she continued, as if Brad's disappearance from the screen meant that he couldn't hear. "I was really despairing of you ever finding a husband. Never would I have imagined not only that you'd find one, but that you'd also find a gem like him."

Sonia smiled at her Wonderful-Mr.-Wilson, who loved her more than she had ever thought a man could. After the night at the crater, Brad had finally felt that he had expiated his sins and extinguished his debt, and he had decided to return to his surgical career. Knowing how much Sonia's job meant to her, he had taken an extended paternity leave to look after Emma while Sonia returned to the classroom. So much for Sonia's paranoia about marriage destroying her career… "Yes, I'm really lucky to have Brad, but him staying at home with Emma is the least of his virtues."

"Of course. He also helps out with the housework."

"Yes, he does, but that's still not why I married him. Sorry, but I've got to go now."

"Go, Soniuccia. And remember that your father and I are proud of you."

"Thank you, Mamma. I love you. Bye."

"Bye." Her mum's chubby smile lingered on the screen. "Er… Could you close the call? I don't know yet how to do it."

Sonia smiled and hung up, then turned to her beautiful daughter and husband. Emma looked so safe and loved in Brad's arms that Sonia couldn't imagine a better father for her baby — or a more tender one — just as she couldn't fathom a more loving husband, a more pyrotechnic lover or a more loyal friend. She took a couple of steps closer, kissed her baby's forehead and her husband's lips.

"Now I'm ready."

Want to see more like this?
Here's a taster for you to enjoy!

Fuel to the Fire
Kait Gamble

Excerpt

Jackie got out of the cab and took a moment to stare at the magnificent hotel. Right away just gazing at the building, she knew that her stay here would be something different. Instead of towering into the sky, the hotel sprawled up the mountainside and outward to the limits of her peripheral vision. The stone façade might as well have been hewn from the rock face while the lush greenery threatened to envelop the entire thing and reclaim it for Mother Nature. The hotel appeared so incredibly natural it could have been a part of the mountain itself.

On the other side, clear blue water lapped at immaculate white sand dotted with brilliant vermillion umbrellas and wooden loungers she couldn't wait to try out.

Magnificent.

In a slight daze, she walked into the grand foyer and out of the sultry air to take a deep breath of the chilled, perfumed interior. Her kitten heels clicked along the stone floor as she gazed at the beautiful architecture and design. The abundance of stone and wood gave the space an organic feel. Dominating one of the walls, a waterfall splashed, surrounded by indigenous plants and a pool where colorful fish flashed in the water. Together with the enormous windows and natural light, the room exuded the perfect relaxed island ambience.

It felt good—great—to be somewhere different. She couldn't remember the last time she'd been on a trip anywhere, let alone somewhere so opulent.

"Jackie! You made it!"

A slender, elegant blonde figure dashed toward her. She was quickly engulfed by the well-toned arms of her best friend, Caroline.

She hugged her friend back. It had been too long. Jackie stepped away to smile at Caroline. "Of course. You didn't think I would skip out on your wedding, did you?"

"It never crossed my mind." Brilliant green eyes sparkling, she wound her arm through Jackie's and led her through the hotel. "Ever been here?"

Jackie grinned up at the luxurious surroundings and shook her head. "No. it's always been on the bucket list, though." The beautifully lush island of St. Lucia was the complete opposite of her everyday life.

Caroline grinned. "I'm glad." Her smile softened. "It really is wonderful to see you. Things haven't been the same without you."

A pang of emotion Jackie didn't want to name twinged in her chest. The first of many times this weekend, she was sure. "Things have been a bit different, haven't they?"

"Head's up." Caroline nodded, her attention on someone behind Jackie.

Jackie had a fraction of a second to brace herself before the group of women was upon them.

"Jaqueline Pennington! I thought it was you!" Regina, Caroline's mother, sashayed up to Jackie with her arms out swept. But instead of a hug, she clasped her by the shoulders and air-kissed her at each cheek. She stepped back to give her a critical once-over, making Jackie glad she had primped at the airport before getting in the cab. Though, from the thinly veiled disapproval in the woman's eyes, Jackie didn't quite make the cut. "My, you have changed! They have a spa here that's supposed to work wonders."

Ignoring the last comment, Jackie flipped her ponytail over her shoulder as she forced herself to smile at the well-coiffed woman and her friends. "It has been a few years, hasn't it? They have been kind to you, haven't they?" Not enough, by Jackie's reckoning. "We should go to the spa together and have a nice long chat and really catch up."

The older woman's expression grew pinched at the insinuation that she would need such a long session, but she quickly recovered. "We're all so glad you're here." She looped Jackie's arm through hers and started walking.

Caroline gave her a helpless shrug and a pleading smile. It was her friend's wedding weekend, and Jackie refused to do anything that would ruin it.

"I saw your mother just the other day. She's doing well. She tells me that she and your father are heading to Rome this summer."

All the muscles in her body contracted at the mention of her parents. She'd known someone would bring them up sooner or later, but she'd hoped it would have taken longer than five minutes after she arrived. "That's nice," Jackie said as mildly as she could.

"It is. They've done quite a bit of traveling, from what I've heard."

Jackie really had no comment about that, so she stayed silent. Focusing on the scenery was much more interesting than listening to Regina blather on about her parents.

"Mum, it's been a while since Jackie and I have seen each other. I wanted to spend some time together before everything starts."

Regina slowed to a stop. "Yes, of course! Silly me!" She spun Jackie into Caroline's arms. "Dinner is at eight." And with that, she flitted off leaving a thick wake of Chanel No. 5.

They watched her until they were sure she was out of earshot.

Caroline smiled apologetically. "Sorry about that. Mum didn't think you would come, and I don't think she quite knows what to say."

Regina hadn't been the only one not to know if she was going to make it. "It's fine. I doubt I'd know what to say either."

Her friend didn't look convinced. "You know, if money is a problem, my offer to pay for your stay still stands."

How had she managed to have such a good friend? "Thanks. But I'm okay—at least for the moment." She laughed weakly. "I highly doubt I'll make use of the magical spa they have here, though."

Caroline joined her in her mirth. "It can't be that great. Otherwise, Mum would never leave it."

Jackie inhaled the fragrant air again and felt her muscles slowly unknot. It had been a long flight and she'd been tense worrying about the kind of reception she'd get. She had expected an inquisition, so she was relieved at how things had fared so far.

She had an entire week to make it through yet.

Caroline led her to the reception and stood by as Jackie went through the formality of checking in.

"We had a minor disaster thanks to one of the groomsmen getting into a skiing accident last week. Charles assures me that he's found a suitable replacement and that he will be here today so you won't have to walk down the aisle alone."

The last thing she was worried about was walking down the aisle solo. "It's lucky you found someone on such short notice." Jackie barely remembered the days when she could drop everything at a moment's notice to do whatever she liked.

Jackie was dimly aware of masculine voices heading toward them. Two of them sounded familiar. She knew Caroline's fiancé, Charles. They'd met a few times before. A Sutcliffe through and through, he was tall, broad, golden blond and blessed with a knack for finances like the rest of his dynasty. It was his laugh that she was able to pick up on immediately.

But the other voice…

Home of Erotic Romance

Sign up for our newsletter and find out about all our romance book releases, eBook sales and promotions, sneak peeks and FREE romance books!

About the Author

Stefania Hartley, also known as The Sicilian Mama, was born in Sicily and immediately started growing, but not very much.

She left her sunny island after falling head over heels in love with an Englishman, and she's lived all over the world with him and their three children.
Having finally learnt English, she enjoyed it so much that she started writing stories and nobody has been able to stop her since.

he loves to write about hot and sunny places like her native Sicily, and she especially like it when people fall in love.

Her short stories have been longlisted, commended and won prizes. *Sun, Stars and Limoncello* is her first novel.

Stefania loves to hear from readers. You can find her contact information, website details and author profile page at https://www.totallybound.com

Lightning Source UK Ltd.
Milton Keynes UK
UKHW041120070221
378372UK00001B/44